Mercy ~ Book 1   Lucian

MERCY

A Dark Erotica

By Lucian Bane

© 2015 by Lucian Bane

All rights reserved. No part of this document may be reproduced or transmitted in any form or by any means, electronic, mechanical, photocopying, recording, or otherwise, without prior written permission of Lucian Bane or his legal representative.

To all the readers, fans, and or reader's clubs. Thank you for supporting my work. I'd also like to ask nicely that you please not Pirate my work. That basically means don't give it away just because you bought it. If you know of anybody that can't afford a copy, just let me know. I'm a nice guy. ☺

Also, if you need a different format, please contact me, the author.

Dedication

Mercy ~ Book 1   Lucian Bane

This book is dedicated to my beautiful, amazing, gorgeous wife. I love you forever. Thank you so much for putting up with me, for believing in me, for loving me.

Acknowledgements:

First, to all the beta readers. We tried, lol. Thank you for whatever you were able to do. Next time will go much better.

I'd like to thank the ladies in my private Dark Erotica group for helping me pick out details on our characters and what-not: **Louisa Gray** Angel wings tattoo. **Syrina Roberts**~ kitchen and bath. **Sherri Maughan** ~Special Room. Mushy Romance book, and For The Love of Pain Thunderclap, **Nan DeVore-Lindsey**~Car, **Jenny McKinney Shepherd**~ Living Room, **Kelly Mallett**~eye contact, **Louisa Gray's Husband**~ Black Velvet, **Jan Kinder**~ Sade's Skin Sanctuary, **Tammy Singleton Burch**~ Sweetest piece of candy in the factory, **Lacy Cosme**~ The Pain Seekers by Lady Dom (Erotic Horror)

A very huge and special thanks to my PA, Jan Kinder. As usual, it would be *oh holy shit* if it weren't for you helping me every single day. All day. And night. The Brat Keeper.

Thank you to my street team, ladies you rock. Every day. Thank you for putting up with all my crazy marketing schemes and endless groups. I love all of you and all the hard work you put out. Seriously.

A special thanks to Kimie Sutherland and team. Kimie, thanks for taking the time to beta read, and thanks to those on your team that help get Mercy into the hands of readers. Big hugs ladies.

Chapter One

Jay shuffled on his feet, his face a disgusting mask of punk. "Man, come on, please! Tommy… he's the one to do this, I'm no good at this!"

Sade grit his teeth, his need for vengeful pain plowing through him with every breath, every second. He needed to punish and demolish, and he needed it now. "Take them!" He shoved the giant dude, pressing the knuckle busters into his chest. "I'm not fucking waiting for Tommy! I'll kill you right here in this alley if you don't do it—now!" he roared.

"Alright man!" Jay's beefy hands shot up, trembling as he took the brass knuckles.

"You're fucking crying?" Sade shook his head in awe. "Jesus you're a goddamn pussy."

"I'm sorry man," he blubbered, fitting the metal onto his fingers, "you know I'm not a coward! But you're my friend."

"Then do it!" Sade ripped off his shirt and pounded his own chest and slapped his face. "Fucking tear it up! If I can recognize myself in the mirror when I wake up" he aimed a finger at him, "I'm coming—and I'm going to show you how it's done, Jay. You don't want that, you're a fucking good looking dude."

Jay shook his head rapidly. "I got you man, I got you. I'll fuck you up good."

God, he was a fucking blubbering whale—tears soaking his face, fucking little bitch. He was adding the wrong kind of fury to an already fucked up day. And Tommy? That two ton sack of shit was going to get it. Not being here on this day when he knew the drill, he fucking knew.

"I need the bathroom man," Jay whimpered.

Sade slammed his fists into the wall of muscle. "Piss in your goddamn pants!" he yelled.

Jay finally nailed him one. Not at full power but it was that first rush, a blessed start!

"Don't stop!"

Jay let out a series of pathetic wails and lit into him. With every pop on Sade's face, fresh life entered him like a cleansing breath. All year a filthy evil built inside his body, and every year on this day, he cleaned that fucking clock. Every year, he threw blood money at a toll that could never be paid, torched a bridge that refused to burn.

But it was another year down. He'd lost track of them. Happy Birthday mom.

*****

Project Johnathon Lee Ashcroft, AKA Sade. That answered a lot for Mercy. Including why her father might not tell her about this. He was too protective. Anything that was connected to danger was off limits to her.

Dizziness swam through her and she sat down with the strange orange envelope that had suddenly popped up out of nowhere two weeks after her father died. It was nothing but past demons attempting to steal the one good thing she'd ever had in her life. Her dad was a mercenary. A mercenary of goodness, that's what he was. And if he was connected to this… criminal looking person in anyway, it was to help him. No doubt about it. Just as he'd done when he rescued her.

The dense pain of the last two weeks eased suddenly as she leaned back and stared at the picture of this Sade person. He had homegrown monster written all over him. It wasn't just the short cropped hair, the tattoos and piercings, or the six foot heavily muscled frame, it was his background. Raised in the worst part of the city, son of a man who dealt in illegal drugs, prostitution, and flesh trade. His mother was murdered when he was four. She scanned for details, not finding any. But it seemed clear that life became a field of blood for him ever since. Did he love her? Remember her? Was she good to him? Bad to him?

Mercy sighed, her heart tight and heavy. He was the saddest form of victim turned criminal with sadomasochism as his only accomplishment to show for it all. She stared into the hard gaze of the man in the picture, wondering about his life and what brought him to that. She tried to imagine him with a smile, what those eyes might look like before he'd turned hard.

Just what did her father have in mind for him was the question.

She tossed the papers onto the couch as the weight of her father's death swept in with its daily blow. She missed him so bad. The grieving process had barely begun and the knowledge that she had months, maybe years of that left, twisted the knife in her heart and stomach. The temptation to go numb and cover it all up stole her breath some days. Sheer will of obligation. That was the life preserver she clung to. Everything her father was and everything he'd sacrificed. The years he'd spent dragging her through recovery, helping her overcome the nightmares and demons of her life—from birth to the time he snatched her out of that fire. The years he spent training her to be strong, equipping her with every manner of self-defense so that nobody could ever hurt her again.

That's why she kept going. That's why there was no giving up. She lived for him now, the way he once lived for her.

She needed to find out what he had in mind with this man. If he'd wanted to help him... then she did too. She could do it.

****

Mercy found a spot to park, not far from the family's club they ran according to Mr. Sade's bio. She argued with the voice of her father about coming to one of the worst parts of Los Angeles in the name of helping anybody, let alone the son of a major drug dealer, illegal arms pusher, and flesh trader. The rogue otherworldly connection with her dad was odd but comforting. In fact, it was the first time she felt alive since he had died.

She stood next to her inconspicuous black Juke, dressed in matching inconspicuous athletic gear. Instincts from years of training mingled with realism, forming a calming concoction. There was no sane reason in the vicinity to be calm. Could have been the adrenalin mixed with feelings connected to her father that caused the misfiring of intuition.

Gripping her collapsible titanium walking stick slash ass beater, she hit the alarm on the car and headed toward the backside of the club. She'd done a bit of recon on the place and there should be an entrance in the alley behind it. And for some reason--maybe her lack-luster social skills--it seemed safer than the front side. It would be her first miscalculation.

The crowd in the front was vanilla ice cream in comparison to the crowd in the back and the energy screamed 'welcome to your last wrong turn'. Her walking stick suddenly felt all wrong too. She clicked the button on top and collapsed it to billy club size while praying it wouldn't be interpreted as a challenge. She was just a nobody pedestrian taking a short-cut through Hell Street. That's all.

Even as she prayed for invisibility, a voice slurred from somewhere too close behind her, "Hey, where you going in such a hurry?"

A shot of panic quickened her legs to the pace of her hammering heart while the instinct to avoid a fight burned in her muscles. No running. Not here. Worst possible confrontation instincts kicked in now, dictating one goal. Do what it takes to survive. No different than training. That's all. All the same. Ass kicking was kicking fucking ass no matter what ground you stood on.

Mercy aimed her momentum for what should be the alley leading to the back entrance. Too bad it was flanked by a large group of people. Only consolation was the mixed gender. Surely it couldn't be worse than who now followed with kissy noises and vulgar laughter that promised fun times in your worst nightmare.

When it was time to ask permission to get through the throng, she clicked the button on the stick and expanded it with a discreet shake. Holding the weapon against her, she rotated the tips between bodies, maneuvering them out of her way with an unnoticeable push and pull. Seconds later, she'd zigzagged right through the small cracks she created and exited the other side.

"Hey! Stop!" a voice yelled behind her as she hurried along. The run instinct hit again and she didn't deny it. With all she had,

Mercy sprinted around that final turn and raced down the stretch with pursuing feet pounding behind her.

Dread slammed her at spotting a barricade at the far end. Don't stop, don't stop.

She flew past a large dumpster, frantically searching the building for some other escape as a deep voice continued to yell stop behind her.

She finally made it to the back entrance of the club and slammed into it. Locked!

A sound of struggling and grunting spun her around where two men fought on this side of the dumpster. Gasping for wind, she looked around the large metal container and found her pursuer pacing in the alley a ways back like he wasn't allowed beyond that point.

The sick smacking of fist on flesh drew her attention. Her gaze zeroed in on the blood covering every inch of the man's face and detonated past nightmares. All her survival training and instincts kicked in again, a singular mantra booming in her blood and pulse. Stop! Stop! Stop! "Stop killing him! Stop it!" she screamed, rushing toward them.

But the beast didn't stop. He beat the lifeless man, giving a cry of torment with every blow. The gleam of brass knuckles caught Mercy's eye and without thought or warning, she swung her stick full force behind the maniac's kneecaps, laying him on his back. She followed with four swift blows-- shins--kidney--diaphragm--trachea--busting them.

The huge man groaned in agony and choked while Mercy knelt next to the bloodied guy and pressed two trembling fingers into his warm neck. No pulse. "Oh God! Sir! Sir, can you hear me?" She fought back her past hysteria clawing to take control of her mind. "I'm sorry," she whispered. She glanced down the alley and caught sight of the man who'd chased her. "Help me! Call 911! Help me!"

"Who... the fuck are you?"

She jerked to the rasp on the ground. "Oh my God, you're alive!" she whispered. "Can you move? I don't have my phone." Her voice shook in relief while feeling like such a fool for not bringing it. "You need a doctor."

"Are you... an angel?" he barely managed through his swollen lips, sounding confused.

"I'm a nurse." She didn't need an x-ray to see it. "You're broken. He broke a lot of fucking bones," she whimpered, staring at the horribly swollen face.

"Really?" The word slurred, sounding oddly hopeful. "Jay... did a... pretty good job."

She stared at him for endless seconds and the realization bashed into her like a tidal wave. Oh my God. It's him. She'd nearly spoken his name and caught herself. "What do you mean?" were the only words she could manage, tiny and hoarse. He knew the guy that beat him? What kind of sick party had she stumbled into?

He attempted to sit up much to her shock and she hurried to help him only to have him resist. "You are not getting up without help."

He paused only briefly and she winced when he smiled with swollen lips. "Yes ma'am."

"Jesus Christ you're so beat up," she muttered, putting her weight into supporting him. "You need a doctor."

"Lead me in," he barely said.

"That door is locked." He stumbled and she put more weight under his arm.

"Lead… me to it."

When they stood at the back entrance, he swayed for several moments with his eyes swollen shut. "Knock," he croaked. She banged on the door rapidly and it opened so quickly, she jumped.

"Ah shit," the deep voice said from the other side. "It's over?"

What's over?

"Leave," he mumbled.

"Me?" she asked.

"Yeah," the deep voice said. "You. Go."

The man pushed her out of the doorway and shut it, leaving Mercy in the alley with the now growling giant behind her. She looked back the way she'd come, finding it empty. Freedom. Her cue. She sprinted the entire way back to her car, busting through people without thought.

No more. She'd seen enough. Done enough. For now.

Back in the safety of her locked vehicle and nearly home, she began to tremble. Wow. What. A fucking. Rush. She'd met Sade—be it unofficially. What a mess. What in God's name was he doing-- what in the hell was going on in that alley? Some kind of initiation? He was kind of... owning everything to be doing anything crazy like that though wasn't he?

So many more questions now. So many sad questions. But... she had reason to make contact again. Shit. How the hell would she legitimately have his number? Dammit!

She remembered the mention of a tattoo shop that he owned in his bio. That was it. That was her next lead. She would check that door and see if it led inside.

Chapter Two

Four days of recuperation. Sade wasn't happy with that. Should have been more. Fucking pussy Jay. He stood at the stainless steel fridge, a flash of a face surfacing. He had dreamed of a girl. He thought harder and remembered only worried green eyes. Was it somebody he knew? Maybe someone from his past? Had he come close enough to dying that he saw angels? He snorted. Dying. Joke of his life. Death was the biggest fucking temptress whore. He didn't fuck many things but he'd fuck death right in its loud-ass mouth.

She may have been pretty like an angel but he was sure no angel would ever come to his aid for any fucking thing.

The sound of the phone drew his gaze toward a too bright living room. He made his way over and peered down at the number. Out of state. Probably a telemarketer. He headed back to the kitchen for that protein shake. Time to get back in the game. Play the play and work for the fucking man.

Twenty-five couldn't come fast enough. One more year and he'd be free of his bastard father.

The answering machine clicked on. "Hey Sade, sorry about the no show. I'm calling from Mexico man, I ran into some trouble."

Sade hurried to the phone as fast as he could at hearing Tommy's odd voice. He yanked the receiver up. "Tommy?"

"Sade, man. Look, I got trouble."

Sade's heart hammered at the finality in his tone. "Talk to me."

"It's over for me man. I'm just calling to let you know. I crossed some lines. I got one call to make. Look, don't worry about it," he said lightly, sympathy in his voice.

Sade clenched his eyes shut, already knowing. Tommy had finally gotten caught dipping. He fucking knew he would. He was right, there was not a damn thing he could do and yet... "I got money."

"Aw man," he sounded grateful. "No way out of this. And you told me, you tried to warn me. I just wanted to say…" Sade held his breath during the long pause. "I love you like a brother." Those final words were nearly whispered and not easily spoken he knew. "Was real good knowing you. I'm sorry I wasn't there for your mom's birthday man, you know I was always there for you."

Sade's jaw refused to unhinge for him to speak. Speak final words to a man he was only a half-ass friend to. He was trapped in that prison of silence, the fucking place he cowered with his arms over his head so the pain could have its way. Sometimes you had to let go and not fight, some pains you couldn't fight, they were bigger than you. Those times Sade prayed two things. That he'd die, or that he'd live stronger. And since he was still living, he was one strong motherfucker. But this…. This pain was different.

"I hear you man," Tommy whispered. "Even though you can't say it. But I gotta go now."

The phone disconnected and the receiver trembled in Sade's death grip. His eyes remained clenched tight as the monster inside him made its way through the cracks in that vault door. And when it finally plowed through, Sade opened himself wide for it, devouring its rage and demolishing his entire condo and everything in it. Destroy, kill, destroy, kill. It was all there was. All there ever was.

And there was no more Tommy.

****

Sade made his way to the shop, the urge to give and receive pain in a vicious tug-of-war inside him, a steady pulse in his body. It all had his sick dick hard like iron as he entered the shop from the back, hoping nobody was there and yet praying they were. Everything was a conflict inside him, from what he needed and wanted to how he'd go about getting it.

The idea of seeing another human added to his hungry fury, which in turn added to his need for a brutal fight. But that was still two days out, or two fucking years if you asked his desperation.

He got to the front of the small store and found it empty. Any relief that might have given him was sucked up by his need for confrontation of any kind. He checked the schedule, hoping to find it empty, hoping he'd be driven to desperate measures. Do it life. Just fucking do it, make me. Make me break.

The phone rang as if in answer to the direct challenge and he jerked it off the receiver. "The Triple S," he half growled.

"Uhhh, yes, I was calling to schedule an appointment for a tattoo?"

Sade thought the voice sounded familiar. "I'm open, what do you want."

Again he expected fate to kick him in the balls with some pissy five minute job. He needed a fifteen hour job, something he could get saturated in.

"Well, I've never had a tattoo before," she said, making him roll his eyes. "How long does it take?"

"Depends on what you get," he said pissed. "The bigger and more complex the tattoo, the longer it takes."

"Hmm. Do I pick something you have or can I bring my own picture that I want?"

"I do customs for an extra charge. But depending on what you have, I might be nice."

"Oh," she said, sounding intrigued. "How long would it take to do one that covers my entire backside?"

Desire slammed his balls at his shocking good fortune. "Depends on the image."

"Wings," she said with a dreamy sounding sigh. "I think I'd like to be an angel."

An angel. How quaint at such a fucking time. "Wings." The idea of the long, agonizing work appealed to his masochistic need but not as much as having this ignorant, vanilla sounding blonde on his table for hours in agony.

"What? Is that too hard?"

"Not at all. But you should know it could take hours."

"I have time."

"As in twelve. And I only break to eat and release." And he didn't mean take a piss. Not wanting to lose the customer, he threw in, "But I'd make an exception if you came in today since I have no other work."

"Okay perfect," she said, sounding as elated as his dick felt. "Do I need to bring anything with me? Aspirin? For the pain?"

"Nope. Just yourself. And two hundred dollars." A seventy percent discount.

"Whoa that's steep. Glad I saved for a rainy day."

Yeah, because it's pouring down sunrays outside. "And cash only."

"Got it. On my way. My name is Mercy, by the way. And should I bring lunch? Guessing yes."

Sade closed his eyes, hating the desperate low he'd just stooped to. And with a woman named *Mercy* of all fucking things. "Whatever." And say hello to the ass it always made him into. He wasn't bad at very many things, but controlling his temper and tongue with the general public was his prized weakness. It was just too easy to beat a motherfucker in the face without the least thought for him.

****

Mercy drove to the tattoo shop, arguing with the voice of her father again. All along the lines of she needed to stop, she was taking this too far, etc. etc. But how else would she get to know the man? This was it. It was a tattoo. She'd wanted a tattoo most of her life anyway. Sure, angel wings covering her entire back was crazy, she could consent to that much. But she wanted something that took enough time to get plenty of information without looking like she was digging.

She just hoped it didn't hurt too badly. She'd googled it. Felt like cat scratches. That was nothing, it would probably feel good to her considering her pain tolerance levels. A perk coming from a life of abuse followed by intense physical training in Wing-Chun.

Not wanting to give him a sexual impression, she dressed in her depressing yoga monk outfit with the pants and top that could pass for a long dress. It had been a little under a week since that night and she worried a little about what he'd look like, or worse, that he'd recognize her.

Really, if he recognized her, that wasn't a big deal. Except what was she doing behind the club? She could say she got lost or something.

Already she was shocked he'd answered the phone. She was expecting to talk to a receptionist not him. And now she was headed over there to get a tattoo that would take twelve hours. Plenty of chat time.

She parked near the family BDSM club next to the tattoo shop, glad to be going in from the front this time, and in the daylight. She half ran the quarter block to her destination, feeling like something might happen to ruin her good fortune if she didn't hurry and seize it. Like karma would cut in and say sorry, too slow.

Opening the door, she walked in and slid her sunglasses to the top of her head, pushing the hair out of her eyes as she made her way to the small counter. Was like a dark little closet in there. She set her black leather purse on the tiled top, looking around at the scheme of dark contrasting colors and abstract lines. Hmm. Somebody paid a decorator.

Behind the counter a collage of photos with people showing off their tattoos filled the entire wall save one single black door. She scanned the individuals in the pictures, some scarier than the freaky tattoos they bore. Did he do all those? Wow, he was talented. She angled her head at the dude with a werewolf climbing out of his back. It looked so real, like the flesh was actually bloody and torn. She eyed the door briefly as she got out the wing design she'd decided on. And the message she wanted between the wings.

The door opened and her stomach tensed as he emerged. Wow, she didn't remember him being so big. But his size was a peripheral notation compared to the discoloration on his face as he approached in a tight black t-shirt. He was definitely into fitness.

"Was in a little accident," he said.

Mercy realized her alarm showed. But then anybody would have that reaction, especially somebody who didn't know about the incident, as she shouldn't. "Wow," she said. "I'd hate to see the windshield. I'm Mercy. Oh yeah, I told you that on the phone already."

He chuckled a little and she noticed he still miraculously seemed to have all his teeth. "Yeah. Sade. I don't think I gave my name."

"Hi. Oh," she said, getting to the reason she was there. "This is the picture I'd like done." She unfolded the paper and slid it to him. "And these words as well. In between the wings." She pointed to the writing. "Center of my back?"

He nodded, staring at it. "Do you know what kind of font that is?"

"Font?" she looked at it. "Oh, that's my handwriting."

He shrugged a little. "I can try to match it."

"Whatever font is easiest is fine."

He nodded then looked at her. "So you want the wings over your entire backside."

"Entire back, yes."

He paused for a moment. "You said backside on the phone."

She pursed her lips in confusion and concern. "Uhhh. I meant… entire back… side. Yeah I can see how you misunderstood. Wouldn't that be… too much?"

"Too much what?"

"Work for you?"

"Not at all, everything is ready. Ink amounts mixed and prepared."

Ooookay. She shrugged, not missing his perturbed tone like he wouldn't be happy if she changed her mind. "That works. Oh shit."

He paused, eyeing her.

"I'm guessing I'd have to… undress for that." Wow no-no-no. She hadn't thought of that. The back was one thing, she could cover her front. But her scars.

"Yeah?" Like he wasn't getting the problem. Of course he wasn't, he did this all the time. "Look," he said. "This is my job. An ass is an ass, they're all the same to me. I don't even like them, honestly."

Oh wow. He sounded quite convincing. No doubt lying, but convincing. An ass was an ass. "Okay then. I'm a nurse, so I get that."

He paused for a moment, seeming to recall something. Mercy panicked for a second before he walked off. "Follow me through that side door."

She glanced to the wall on her left and spotted it hiding in the abstract designs. Hurrying over, she entered a little hall just before a large room with a black, bed type table.

"Go ahead and remove your clothes in the bathroom on your left, and wrap yourself with the sheet provided."

His voice sounded like it came from somewhere in that room. Mercy slipped into the small restroom and shut the door. Lord help her. She hung her purse on the hook behind her and removed the safe monk clothing. Folding all of it and hiding her underwear in between, she set it on a little table in the corner hoping it was okay to put it there.

When she was wrapped in the black sheet, she stared at the door. Just a tattoo. A very long one. Just an ass. Just a boring ass out of a thousand others.

She opened the door, not letting herself think about him staring at her butt for all those hours or what he'd think of the scars there. She'd be willing to trade sordid stories if he was. There was always that.

Chapter Three

Sade stepped into his private office to change into work clothes, which consisted of tight spandex briefs under loose fitting pants to hide his raging erection. Most of his customers knew him and he was sure a lot knew of his sexual kinks by now but this was a legitimate client.

His little explosion at his condo had helped curb his appetite, but thoughts of Tommy between now and then—namely the times Sade had been a dick to him—had him back to square fucking one.

"What's in there?"

Sade turned from his table of tools and found his nosy customer staring through the one-way glass window leading to his special tattoo room. The sheer lust of wanting to work in that room prevented him from saying what he should have. *It's not your concern* "It's a special tattoo room."

He was willing to see if she was one of those women who played socialite by day, kink-goddess by night. He could always stand to have a few more of those on standby for the rare but inevitable sexorcisms. They usually only happened once a year and he paid the most seasoned whores well for it. During those episodes, his sadism thrived on breaking them sexually. Some would think a seasoned whore couldn't be broken but they could. He went until he felt it in their bodies, heard it in their voices. He went until there was blood, and he didn't stop until he got it. The sexorcism could take hours before his sadism was satisfied which is why he used more than one woman, to avoid killing them. And while his masochism held it at bay, sometimes his sadism won, sometimes that demon would pick the lock and unleash hell for daring to refuse him.

"Oh?" The angelic look she gave him over her shoulder said she was a hundred years away from entering that room. "Like what?"

But he could definitely talk about that room. "Like kinky. Come to the table," he muttered, getting his tools lined up.

"Kinky," she repeated, sounding curious. "What does that mean? I mean in the world of tattooing?"

She stood like a dumb lamb, not moving from where she stood. Sade decided she was either spoiled and use to getting her way, or she was stalling. Either of those poked at both his addictions to the point of annoying. "I give tattoos while the customer is tied up in a painful or humiliating position. Sometimes I use dull needles, depending on my mood."

She approached the table slowly, her eyes wide in what he could only name as fascinated shock. Not the look she should be giving. "Does it hurt really bad? Are you saying you like hurting them?"

Sade was careful to not let on what he was thinking since people used that to their advantage. So did he. And he didn't give over that play to anybody. Her genuine curiosity behind her question coupled with the fact that she seemed to assume he was a nice guy, turned him on as much as it bothered him.

"It hurts as bad as they want it to." He eyed her for a moment, debating on how to answer that second question. Did he want her to be afraid of him, or trust him? "Yes. I like hurting them."

She suddenly went stealth, masking her emotions and Sade found her reaction interesting but he wasn't sure why. "So they like to be hurt and you like to… hurt them?"

He was really surprised she'd turned out brunette. "Everybody likes a little pain sometimes," he said slowly, taking in her body type now, ready to get to work on her. The small frame would take a lot less time. He would have to go slower.

"Is there a problem?"

He raised his gaze to hers. "No, just estimating."

She pointed to the table. "If you don't mind, I'll start with the kiddie tattoo room."

Of course she would. "Remove the sheet." He turned to his tray of tools, his conflicting desires warring like rabid lovers. One was disappointed to hear what he already knew and the other hungry to mar that perfect skin of hers as a punishment. Like a clean, virgin canvas.

She let out a sharp yell and he turned to see her fall from the rolling bed onto the floor.

"Shit." He hurried around to help her up. "My bad, I forgot to lock the wheels. You okay?"

The pink in her cheeks gave his cock a shot of heat while part of him also felt like an idiot. "Runaway bed," she said, pushing hair behind her ear while clutching the sheet to her front.

He went around and locked the wheels and patted the bed. "There you go." Again he went back to his table so she could remove the sheet and hop on. She probably fell trying to get on without removing it.

"Okay," she said, her voice muffled.

"Coming," he muttered, wiping his hands on his cock before turning and standing next to the bed. "First thing I'm going to do is stencil the design onto your body with a pen." Sade used his finger, demonstrating from the top of her shoulders, slowly down. He finally paused at several things. The way she clenched her butt tight when he drew near it, the light squealing noise she made, and the scars on her ass, lower back, and upper legs.

"Is something wrong?" she said in a strained voice.

It was more than he could stand not to. Very softly, he traced a finger over one of the thick scars.

"Excuse you," she jerked her head to him. "What the hell?"

"Sorry," he said, locking his gaze on hers. "I had wagered you had no flaws on your body."

"Wagered with who?"

He answered honestly. "Myself."

"Yeah well. You lost. I got my ass beat a lot when I was young."

"I see that." How very interesting.

"No need to stare," she muttered, putting her head back down and facing away.

More confliction came with her tone. He wished she would behave one way or another so he could choose a need. But it was like she kept dangling bait before both his desires. He wasn't sure why he would want to feel pain around her when her weak nature sucked his cock better than any woman ever could. "Going to be hard not to look."

"Look, but don't stare."

But that's exactly what he did. He stared. At those scars. A dense ache urged him to touch them. Feel the thickness. Gauge the pain. Once again, the need to be punished hit him.

"You can draw now."

He realized she was letting him know it was taking too long. He picked up his pen and glanced at the wing drawing for several seconds and began his outlining. He was supposed to wear gloves but didn't and hoped she didn't call him on it. Placing one hand and forearm on her back, he carefully, and slowly, drew.

"So," she said, attempting small talk. "Is Sade your real name?"

"No," he answered, his cock hard, as his pen approached her ass. "Is Mercy your real name?" His free hand kept pace with his drawing one, a steady brace for leverage.

"Yep."

The fear in her voice gripped his fucking hard-on, much like an eager pussy would. Delicious. He pressed his hard on into the bed and used her ass cheek to brace his free hand on now.

"How long have you been doing this?"

He stifled a grunt at hearing what that touch did. She acted like a fucking virgin. "Since I was fourteen," he muttered. "Do the scars bother you?"

"Nope," she said.

He kept his face close to his work, which meant his breath hit her ass when he talked. "Does it bother you that I'm touching them?"

"Honestly?"

He paused, waiting to see if she'd lie.

"It bothers me a lot. But I know how to deal. Do what you need to."

Her honesty did strange things to him, none that he liked and yet loved. Or was it her courage? He went back to drawing. "You know how to deal, huh?"

"Yep."

"So forthcoming," he murmured.

"I've had training."

"What kind?" He was on her upper thigh and he slid his hand between them. "Need you open just a little."

"Shit," she whispered.

When he realized he wasn't getting off to her reaction, he paused in frustration. "Maybe this was a bad idea. We can stop—"

"No! I'm fine." She opened her legs a tiny bit and Sade gazed at the dark hair on her pussy for several moments. "Now what!" she cried.

"Nothing, sorry. I was looking at the image." But what he was also doing was breathing her in. The scent of a woman's pussy was a turn off—except during those sexorcisms—and he was ready to have control of his cock back. He'd finally chosen his desire. Hurting her. But fuck if she didn't smell different enough to make him fumble that ball.

He turned from the bed, needing to breathe fresh air. He selected another color pen to draw with, getting more pissed by the second with how she was screwing with is controls.

The door opened suddenly and she gasped with a little squeal.

"What the fuck dude?"

"Sorry man," Bo said, sounding surprised before quickly shutting the door.

Of course he was surprised, Sade never reacted to somebody entering his workspace. But this was a legitimate client, he reminded himself.

"Excuse me," Sade said, throwing the sheet over her. "I'll be right back."

She answered with barely a squeak and the intimidated, humiliated sound suddenly infuriated him. Because again, it did nothing for him when it should have.

He went out into the hall and told Bo, "Sorry man, a legitimate customer in there."

Bo pointed at the door. "Her? I'm here to tell you that's her."

"Her who?"

"I just spotted her car outside. I didn't get a chance to tell you yet man, but I was watching the alley that night. You know… that night. She got through and I'm sorry about that. I didn't think nothing of it till Jay told me she was the one that hurt him with a stick that night."

"Jay's hurt?" Sade asked.

Bo's eyes widened and he whispered. "She shattered his shin, busted his kidney and broke his trachea man."

"What?" Sade hissed, his cock waking up again. "She stopped him?"

"Would have to be her. Dumpster was in the way man, it was dark. I couldn't see too good. But I followed her when she left in that car. Got enough numbers on the plate to make sure."

"Who was at the back entrance that night?"

"Sans man. And I checked with him. He said a woman knocked on the door and helped you in."

"Holy fuck," Sade whispered, looking off to the right. "Thought I'd dreamed that. I knew she seemed familiar."

"You were pretty out of it."

"And that's her?" Sade pointed with his thumb to the door, his hard-on raging now.

"Pretty sure," he said. "Could be a huge coincidence but I don't think so."

"How about I let you get a look at her?" And just what the fuck did she want? Was she undercover? "If you're sure it's her, code word 'I'm blue', if
not, 'I'm red'."

"Got it man."

"Give me fifteen minutes and come knock again."

Sade went back into the room and announced, "I'm really sorry to do this, but I'm going to have to reschedule."

She lifted her upper body and pulled the sheet over her breasts but not before Sade caught a glimpse of the outer edge of the tiny mounds. "What's wrong?"

"Personal family crisis." He tossed his thumb at the door. "My father, actually." He helped her stand and wrapped the sheet around her. "I'm really sorry."

"Not at all, of course. Family is most important."

He led her to the bathroom. "We'll reschedule?"

"Of course, absolutely."

She went into the bathroom and Sade paced, thinking. What would an undercover cop want with him? Had to be what she was. There were a million things, but why now? What particular thing?

She exited the bathroom dressed in her nun looking outfit. Right on cue, the other door opened.

"Sorry to bother again."

"No, it's fine Bo."

Bo glanced at the woman for several seconds and looked at Sade and nodded. "I'm very blue."

Sade would have laughed at how stupid that sounded except he was too pissed. "Thanks man. I'll be right there." Fucking shit.

He left and Sade led little Miss Mercy to the front. "When would be a good time for you to come back?"

"Ohhh, anytime," she said lightly.

So accommodating. He'd see about that. She wanted information on something and he'd have to find out what.

"Do I have your phone number?" he asked.

"Ummm, let me give you my cell." She dug in her purse and got a pen.
Biting the cap off she wrote on the card that Sade handed her. "And my home phone too."

Home phone? What kind of stupidity was that? This fucking woman was ruining an already horrible day. "Not a good idea to give your home phone out," he said, putting the card in his pocket.

She waved her hand. "It's actually a satellite phone, it doesn't come with an address. I'm not that stupid," she said with a laugh.

Clearly not since satellite phones were easy to track. Sade was still at plan A. Busting her before she got anything on him.

He may have strange kinks but he still knew when a woman was attracted to him. And she most certainly was. "I'll call you when I'm done with my personal business." He held out his hand and she regarded it, confused before realizing what he wanted.

She thrust her hand out and put it in his and Sade gave it a little shake with a smile.

He was back to extremely fucking hard now with this odd turn of events, and he could hardly wait to map out a game plan with the sweet little Miss Mercy.

****

Mercy drove home, frustrated. So much for that! *I'm very blue. Who was that dude? Why would he say such a... weird thing in front of her? He seemed vaguely familiar. God what if he was one of the men she'd encountered that night?*

I'm so blue, very blue. What did that mean? Seemed very code-ish.

And now she was down to a "Don't call me, I'll call you" scenario. Not that the majority of her wasn't thrilled about getting out of that tattoo, out of all the touching he was doing. Was all that really necessary? Hand on her ass? Face all near her skin like a five-year-old in a coloring book!

She was pretty sure he was getting off too. Looking at the image. Sure he was. She didn't buy that for a second. Touching her scars! More like molesting them. Sick fucker. And yes, she'd hit on his little broken box of naughties right off the bat. He liked to give pain. Just popped right out with it. No shame in his game. Like it was just fine and normal to like to hurt people. Then again, how would he not like to give pain? That was one of the trademarks of a life of abuse. Was he masochistic too? Usually they went hand in hand to varying degrees if she remembered right.

She'd have to break out her psychology materials and freshen up. To know what to look for, what to expect. How to handle it.

Despite her sudden dead end, Mercy was pretty sure she'd never felt more alive in her life. This was just what she needed. To do something good. Not only was it the best form of therapy, it was useful. She enjoyed her work at the retirement homes, helping the elderly, but this… this was different. She was helping change a life maybe. Not preserve what little was left. And she was walking in her father's legacy. That especially was awesome.

Chapter Four

Mercy bolted up in bed to the sound of her phone on the nightstand. Shit, she'd laid down for a nap. She snatched it up and squinted at the screen. Sliding her finger across, she answered, "Hello?"

"Mercy, it's Sade."

The deep low voice made her stomach flip. "Ohhh hey, is everything okay?"

"Everything is fine. Well, actually, it's not. I just found out a friend of mine died yesterday and… it's been rough."

"Oh my God," she whispered. "I'm so sorry to hear that."

"Whatever," he muttered.

"Take your time, the tattoo can wait. Do what you need to."

"I sort of lost my shit at my condo and demolished it. So, I'll be spending a few days cleaning up that mess. You wouldn't happen to know anybody that could stand to make a few extra bucks to help me out?"

"Oh, hmmm," she pretended to think. "Honestly, I could really use the money. Between rent, school and bills, it's tight."

"Really? Are you sure?"

"Absolutely."

"When can you start?"

"Tomorrow, if you need me to."

He hesitated and gave a sigh.

"What's wrong, that too soon? Whenever you need."

"No, actually, family is due in this weekend and I was hoping to start right away. How early can you come in the morning?"

"I can come now if you need, I have nothing to do. You give me the address and I'll be there with a bucket and a bottle of Mr. Clean, no problem."

"I'll pay you extra for the short notice."

"It's a deal," she said, remembering she was supposed to need the money. But she'd really do it for free. In a heartbeat.

He gave her the address and she hung up and googled it real quick.
Wow. He lived in Ridgefield? Go figure.

Mercy got dressed in her regular training clothes. They were all purpose, really. Easy to move in, nothing flashy or too classy. Not the monk type garb she'd worn earlier to the tattoo shop but nothing to take note of either.

She punched his address into the Juke's GPS and listened to some of her father's favorite classical music as she made her way to her destination. He lived in a condo. At least she didn't need to worry about losing her life in this neighborhood.

Okay, show time. She locked up her car and slipped on her shades, ready to tackle a major clean up.

****

Sade had gotten the condo nearly done before Mercy got there. No way could he have her see the place like it was. He didn't need lunatic added to his rap sheet. His mind was nearly in the same state of chaos as his condo. Miss Mercy was playing a game and he needed to get to the bottom of it. Too much of it was new to him. This game. This woman. This threat. At the same time, the danger was irresistible. She was like a sexual wild card. One he knew he could use once he figured out exactly what she was made of. Sade thought about it for a while, trying to remember ever having such a wild card before. He didn't think so.

And oh how sympathetic she sounded. She'd taken his bait like a hungry big mouth bass, giving herself away. He couldn't think of a woman who wanted him for anything but sex or money. And though she was physically attracted to him, that's not what initiated whatever she was up to. And sticking his dick in an electrical socket would be more arousing than the idea of actual sex with her. Except sexorcisms. Always except sexorcisms. His usual rules and preferences didn't apply in those cases. Which is why he loathed them. Being sexually driven to the point of indulging in things he hated on any given day was not something he fucking liked one bit.

He'd stick with the standard for little Miss Mercy. Be it fear, pain, or humiliation, he would have her squirming and writhing, and giving him whatever information he wanted.

The doorbell rang and he tossed the trash bag full of debris aside and headed to answer it. He opened the door and regarded her in this new look. "Miss Mercy." The first thing she hit him with was direct eye contact. Not just direct, but penetrating. Searching. Sincere. It all felt like a challenge to Sade even though he was sure it wasn't. But it challenged him regardless. He found himself very guarded with Miss Clueless for more than one reason.

"You okay?"

Add sympathetic. She was very good with that and it was something Sade wasn't comfortable with. "I've been better." The empty words came with a sweeping gaze over her extremely petite frame. He was again baffled with the idea she'd taken down Jay. Except for the stick and him knowing that the right technique could definitely manage it, he'd never believe it.

The second her eyes left his, she turned into a virgin. Maybe it was the no shirt. And the tattoos. And the piercings. "Wow," she looked behind him.

He stood aside and regarded the remaining mess. "Yep."

She entered and he perused her body as she went. "You get an A for..." she seemed to struggle for a word. "Okay, bad joke. You really lost it."

He shut the door. "Yes I did. You want a drink?"

"You have coffee?"

The selection wasn't a surprise. *Would you like donuts with that, detective?* "I can make some."

"Oh. Nice."

"What, I don't look like the coffee type?"

She gave a little laugh. "Not really, no. More like the triple Red Bull type."

He chuckled with her honesty. He was used to people lying to him for whatever reason. "I'll put on coffee. I hope you like it strong."

"That's the only way to drink it. Tell me what to do, I'll get started."

He thought about that. He suddenly wanted so badly to have a violent
orgasm. "Just have a seat. I'm ready for a break."

"Okay. Where should I sit?"

In his favorite chair in the basement is where he wanted her. Strapped down. Scared. Talking. Telling him what she wanted. "Wherever you want to."

"I'll sit here." She sat on the kitchen stool while he ran down the fixings for coffee. Of which he had none, it would turn out.

"No coffee."

He pulled out two cans of Monster drink and handed her one.

She laughed. "I knew it."

"Did you?"

She popped open the can, nodding while he watched her take a drink. He remembered he had a stash then. And in that stash he had something that might make this night a lot easier.

"You mind if I take a quick shower?"

She shook her head. "Not at all. I'll um…" she looked around.

"Wait for me," he answered.

"Wait. Right. If you insist. Maybe I could kick everything to a corner at least."

"Just wait. If you don't mind."

She shrugged. "No. Do your thing."

"Unless you have to leave soon."

"Nope. I'm off from school and work for a few days."

He nodded. "I have family coming in."

"You said that, right." Her happiness for him made everything awkward, driving all the wrong needs in all the wrong directions. "My dad died about two weeks ago." She nodded, looking around and Sade froze with that random, unemotional, dump of information. "So I get what you're going through. I think." She shrugged and nodded, turning her can. "Everybody processes differently." She gave him a bright smile and boom. It finally happened. His cock hardened like steel.

"I'll go grab that shower." He headed to his room, adrenalin pumping. He located the stash and took one capsule out. He would only need half for her. He tucked it in his pocket and went to the bathroom. Everything had to be clean entering that room, but he would make an exception for Miss Mercy. Not for himself though. While showering, he washed his cock thoroughly, not sure what he might end up doing with her. She had a very unpredictable effect on him and he needed to be ready for what came. And if that was him, he definitely needed to be clean. Judging by the way it throbbed with that mere thought, his body was ready for that. He'd denied himself way past the justified point and his testosterone was at that reversing, shut down level.

Once he released, everything would reset. It always reset things back to the order he was accustomed to, fucked up as it may be, it was his order.

Dressing in spandex underwear and baggy flannel pants, he went out and found her in the kitchen washing dishes. He fetched a bottle of wine from his selection under the snack bar and two glasses.

"Oh, you scared me." She glanced over her shoulder and turned off the water. "Celebrating?"

"Relaxing. Wanna join me?"

"I don't drink," she said, making him straighten. "Hardly," she added. "One drink is fine though."

"One it is," he muttered, setting the glass on the counter. He poured their drinks. "Maybe we can locate the stereo remote so we have something besides silence to clean up to."

"Any particular direction I can look in?"

"Not really, but I'm hoping near the stereo."

****

Poor guy, Mercy thought as she looked through the mess of misery. Really wasn't that bad though. He either didn't have a lot of stuff or he'd never seen a true mess. But still, to think he'd lost his cool to this degree over a friend. That said a lot about him. Good things, she thought. She turned over another empty frame. That was like the third one she'd found. Had he taken the pictures out before she got here? Surely he didn't keep empty frames around.

How sad that would be. What would it mean if he did? That he had no family? Nobody? Or that he hated family and friends? Maybe he just liked the look of the frames. Maybe he thought framing nothing was something. He was a man, hurting, and that wasn't a bad thing either. He needed help learning how to process, that's all. All his signals were crossed and instincts seared from a life of constant pain, betrayal, and anger. She knew what that could do and she knew what it felt like to try and reverse it. It took her many years and she wasn't a lifetime victim. Only half a lifetime.

"Found it," he said. She turned as he aimed it at the stereo and muffled music came on. He grinned. "It's for the one in my bedroom. Good enough." He turned and then walked to the couch and sat, putting her glass of wine on the coffee table before him.

She followed him over and sat, getting her glass and looking around. "It's really not as bad as I thought it was going to be." She took a small sip. Yuck. She was not a drinker and this was why. All booze was nasty to her.

She watched him down his wine and she took a bigger sip of hers. He was numbing out. She knew what that was like too. She stared down into the glass.

"You don't like it? I can get you another kind."

"No, no," she said. "It's fine."

"Not a drinker I see."

There was a tone about him. Like she was just meeting every virgin conclusion he'd drawn. Mercy was not the type to impress anybody and yet… She downed the wine and put the glass on the table, unable to resist a sour face as she swallowed the last bit. "Sorry," she said. "That is clearly nasty." Geeze, she shouldn't have drank so quickly. And… wow, that was good wine.

"You okay?"

She looked at him and the room spun a little. "I'm fine. Just… wow. Drank that too fast I think." Alarm filled her when the dizzy got extremely worse. "Sade?" she looked at him and her fears grew at finding him smiling.

"What?" he asked.

He was… *mocking* her. Oh dear God. Panic punched through her body and Mercy launched off of the couch only to fall into the coffee table when her legs lagged behind. She struggled and hit the floor, barely missing a face plant. Her head weighed a ton as she crawled, not sure where she was going. "Sade," she whispered before collapsing.

****

Sade carried Mercy to his perfectly sterilized workroom in the basement. She smelled clean, thankfully.

He looked around, thinking. Where did he want her? Considering she might be out for a while, he laid her on the chair that could also convert to a bed. The restraints would prevent her from falling off and injuring herself.

"S-s…"

Was she trying to say his name still? Odd that she'd want to. Her tone was interesting to him, like she was sure he didn't mean any of it. Maybe her mind was stuck on the last thing it was able to logically do-- reason with him.

He held her face in his hand and turned it to him. "Mercy," he said quietly. "I'm going to let you sleep a bit and then we're going to have a little talk." He slid his thumb on the soft skin of her cheek and then let his hand glide off.

Sade got her keys from her bag on the counter and drove her car to a parking garage a few blocks over. He dug through the car for anything telling about the mysterious Mercy, listening to the music playing. Classical. Not a bit surprised with the taste.

She was a sloppy person, but at least clean. He pocketed all the paper items except what needed to stay, locked up, and jogged back home.

Locking the door, he walked over to the couch and plopped down with his findings. First thing he went through was the address book on her phone. A couple of male names, mostly female. A few places of business. He then went through her texts, finding far too little. No doubt this was all a front. Nobody had this much of no life. Especially a woman with her looks and charm.

The receipts showed she bargain shopped. Not surprised. But again, everything on the receipts were too normal. Hair products, school items. Aha. He stared at the receipt that told him what he needed to know. Gun range. Hello detective Mercy.

Sade put all her shit in his vault in the basement then finished cleaning his condo. He didn't like that he had the urge to check on her every few minutes. He needed to get to the bottom of the Mercy mystery and be fucking done. If this had anything to do with that hit-and-run, he'd be in deep shit. Because Tommy was the one driving and now he's fucking dead and couldn't testify for him, should he need.

Jesus Christ, or it could be any number of drug offenses. Or maybe she was trying to get a lead on the underground fights. He needed to know at least *what* she wanted.

Sade bolted up from the couch at the muffled sound of his name. She must be screaming bloody murder for him to be able to hear it. Fuck, was he going to have to gag her?

He raced to the basement and found a very awake Mercy, yanking at her restraints and letting out a bloodcurdling scream that hammered his balls each time.

He grabbed hold of her face and tapped it, making her focus. "I'm right here. Hey!"

"What…" she blinked and furrowed her brows. "Sade," she gasped. "What the fuck are you doing, Sade? Why are you doing this?"

He could hardly believe how gullible and naïve she acted. He turned and pulled up his stool and pumped the lever with his foot, putting him near eye level with her. "Talking to you."

"Why? Why did you do that? You didn't need to do that Sade. I would answer anything you asked me, why are you treating me like a… a criminal?"

He slowly smiled and wagged his finger at her. "You're good detective."

"D… What? Detective? What are you talking about?"

"Look," he held up his hands. "If I'm all wrong, you will have to pardon my manners. But I do have a few issues that I need answers to."

"Like what?"

"Like what were you doing in my alley that night?"

She stared at him with mouth open. "I was… running from some perv!"

He nodded. "That alley was blocked off."

"I only saw a crowd."

"And nobody tried to prevent you?"

She sat with her mouth open a second. "Yes but I was scared. I thought he was just another perv. And then I was at a dead end and I saw you getting killed. Maybe you should be thanking me for happening along—I did save your life!" she reminded.

He winked at her and grinned. "That you did. And why?"

She screwed up her face. "What do you mean why? Because he was killing you."

"And you just happened by?"

She gave a little nod that screamed *lying*. "I'm a very helpful person, my father was the same," she said quietly.

"So what were you even doing there? On my block?"

Her mouth dropped a little then her eyes widened, moving off of him. "I was out for a drive. I got turned around."

Lie. "And so you parked by the Black Velvet BDSM club to get your bearings?"

She rocked a little and shrugged. "I don't get out much and since my father's death I realized it was time."

More lies. "Time to let loose, get into some BDSM?"

"I don't even know what you're saying. BDSM. What is that—body-dancing-something-something? I saw a crowd, and it's not the only club in the vicinity."

Sade took a deep breath. "Your acting skills suck as bad as your lines. How did you know I was going to be in the alley that night, detective?"

She gave him a hard direct stare. "I *didn't*. And I'm not a detective."

He pointed at her. "Now see, you look all honest and even sounded it that time. But it's hard to imagine you just happened to come on the one night of the year where I take care of personal business."

She screwed her face up, confused. "You were getting killed!" Her brows ever so slowly went soft. "Ohhhh," she muttered as though just figuring it out. Her look slowly morphed into horror. "You *made* him beat you nearly to *death?*"

Sade stood now and went to his tray of tools and grabbed a sharp blade. "I'm not here to share what I do with you or why I do it... *detective.* Or pretend that you give a singular shit about that. You're here to share what you want from me."

He turned and wagged the blade at her. "Now, I'm going to play a little game with you called cut away the lies. For every lie you tell me, I cut away clothes until there is nothing left but that pretty skin of yours. And then... if there are still secrets, I'm going to use some of these handy restraints and tie you open. Wide open. Until you are comfortable being transparent with me. And if that doesn't work..." He gave a long sigh and leveled a hard gaze at her. "I have other persuasive tools that will make you talk. Scream even. In pleasure or in pain… it's up to you."

Chapter Five

"I'm not a cop," she swallowed, her words breathy, "or a detective. I work at the hospital, I volunteer at the nursing home. My father died a few weeks ago."

"Ohhhh that. Yes. Your father dying bit." She eyed him with a mix of hope and suspicion. "I do need to verify all of this. His name?"

She drew back a little, looking offended. "I don't see why you need to know that."

Anger shot through him and he grabbed the front of her shirt in one hand and sliced it down the middle with a yank, pulled it entirely off, and tossed it.

"Stop this!" she said.

In answer, he grabbed her bra and cut it the same, tossing it away. "Any other demands, Miss Mercy?"

"You fucking bastard," she whispered pissed.

"I am that, yes. But something tells me you already knew that?" She jerked her gaze away when his eyes lowered to her chest. "Don't worry, your tits don't appeal to me. Now can we have an honest conversation?" It wasn't entirely true about her tits. And it wasn't the size or the look of them that turned him on, it was that they were clearly a vulnerable point for her and the weakness aroused him. If he had to take a guess, it was likely due to how small they were. He noted at that instant one of her nipples was substantially smaller than the other. The defect was delectable to him. Most women assumed big, full, and perfect was the male preference. For him, it was none of that. It was all about perception. Self-perception. "What's the matter Mercy? Are you ashamed of your tits?"

"My shame has nothing to do with how I feel about my tits. *Sade!*"

Damn. She was like the perfect mix of sadomasochistic temptation. "Did you know your anger arouses me almost as much as your weakness?"

She spit at him then turned back to her down and away gaze.

Sade retaliated by going to work cutting off her pants. She screamed loud enough to make his fucking ears ring. After he was done with one leg, he jerked open the drawer below the bed and grabbed the roll of red duct tape. A gag could come later. He ripped off a strip and pressed it to her mouth with a pat then finished cutting off her other pant leg.

He sat back on the stool with a huff. "That didn't take so long. Getting you down to your panties. Black panties." He angled his head, staring. "Nice."

She went back to looking away from him. Judging by the heave of her stomach and chest, she was either very pissed or on the verge of breaking down.

"So detective. What were you doing in the alley that night?"

She jerked her head to him with a mocking look and wide eyes, like *how am I supposed to talk dumbass?* Sade reached over and yanked the tape off. "I'm not. A. Detective!"

Her anger rubbed along his sadism like a stroke on his cock. "The alley, Mercy."

"Already told you, Sade."

"Are you being difficult because you want me to see you naked and wide open? You want me to make you talk? Make you scream?"

He waited in the silence, watching her breaths slow. "I was running from a man. And ended up there. And saved your life! Oh, wait. No, I guess I didn't, I guess I ruined a business deal you had with death?"

He sighed.

"I am *telling* you," she said emphatically.

He leaned forward and grabbed the front of her panties and cut them along both sides and tossed them to the floor. "And I told you not to answer me with the same shit. I don't get it Mercy. Why not just tell me how you know me and why you were there that night?"

"I did and you don't believe me!"

"One more time. Next I help you open up a little more."

"Look! I panicked. I ran. I saw you, I saved you, why am I not getting a reward or something? For good intentions at least!"

He stared at her incredulous. "Jesus," he muttered into the air above as he got up and fetched the rubber restraints.

"I'm telling you the truth!"

"If that's the truth, I feel so fucking sorry for you. It's just too unbelievable." He cut the tie on her ankle, and her legs suddenly clamped around his neck and slammed his face onto the bed-table in a tight choke hold.

"Ffffuck," he growled, reaching with his left hand and pressing her chest. Her pussy almost in tongue touching distance, he grunted in pain and excitement as she choked him harder with solid muscle, screaming with her effort. Her strength was exhilarating. Sade struggled for purchase with his right hand, anything that would give him leverage. But if he made the wrong move, that pressure on his neck would become lethal. He knew that move she was applying all too well.

Sade worked his left hand down her stomach to her pussy. She squeezed his neck harder and he strained with a roar before shoving his thumb inside her.

She gasped and her pussy gripped him while he worked his other hand under her leg, seeking out her sciatic nerve. She struggled and squirmed to maintain her hold, the movement serving as a nice finger job for her and judging by the sounds she made, she didn't get those very often. Sade finally found his target and dug hard. She screamed and he thrust his thumb deeper inside her, gaining that give in her leglock.

He finally broke free and scrambled onto the bed, pressing his knees into her open thighs.

"Mercy, Mercy," he whispered, the smell of her sex everywhere now. She'd gone and done it. Pushed too many wrong buttons. His sadism roared through his blood, begging to take all control. She was back to looking away from him, winded. "I can only assume you wanted that. I do love the fuck out of giving pain and receiving, but only the consenting kind. And that… baby… was very close to begging."

"You're a pig," she whispered. "A disgusting pig."

He kept one of her legs pinned while he carefully restrained the other. Once done, he grabbed hold of the second and restrained it. "Martial arts… I think you forgot to mention that little bit in your resume?"

"My father taught me!" She screamed the words at him. "He was a good man! He saved my life. And I appreciated it!"

"Well," he said, truly surprised. "Somewhat fresh material at least." He sat heavily on the stool, winded and hard as a rock. "Still lame as *fuck* but fresh."

"Do you realize what's going to happen when you let me go?"

"Do tell me," he said eagerly, challenging her with a hungry gaze.

"I am going to… kick your fucking ass, that's what."

Holy fuck, wow. He sat there, truly tickled and happy with what he was discovering with her. "That's it? You seemed like you were going to say something else. And damn I'm tempted to untie you now."

She nodded eagerly. "Oh do it. Please yes. I will kick your ass until you're down for the count, you asshole!"

Asshole. For some reason the term felt endearing, and out of nowhere, a longing hit Sade. "You know. Too bad you're lying."

"Too bad I'm not."

"You and I might actually get along. Be friends even. You're actually fun to be around."

Her anger suddenly dissolved, to his amazement. "Well…" She now debated with herself, transparent as can be. "I mean maybe we still could."

"See, you're still hiding something," he pointed at her.

"Why!?" she said incredulous. "Because I want to be nice and be your friend?"

"Yes!" He stood. "Yes, exactly that! Nobody is my friend, not without a price. The question is, what's yours? Besides gaining your freedom."

She stared up at him, mouth open, eyes locked onto his. "How about a little trust!"

He laughed for a while on that before he got in her face. "You say that like you're so offended that I don't! What fucking planet are you from? Since when do you just *trust* anybody?"

"Okay I get that you wouldn't, given your life."

"Ohhhh." He put a hand on his chest. "My life? What do you know about it? Detective?"

She hesitated a moment, big bad attitude settling down. "I mean it's kind of obvious. You… clearly need help, you pay people to try to kill you. You do understand that's not… healthy in any fashion? Not exactly Sesame Street traits."

He sat back down, ready to consider another angle. Hands on his legs, he angled his head for a hard stare between her thighs. "You know that your pussy is wet?"

She jerked her head to the side now.

"What does that say?"

"That I'm human?" Like he was stupid.

"Yeeees," he dragged out casually, "and that you're arouuuused?"

"Body's react. And your point?"

"When aroused. The question is, what is making your pussy wet?"

"You shoved your thumb in it!"

"It was already soaked when I did that. Had to be something before, I think," he concluded casually.

"Me needing to bust your ass, that's what," she muttered.

"Fuck, you make my cock throb when you talk like that." He sat on the bed to get closer and she looked away more. "So I don't arouse you? At all?" He lowered his gaze to her breasts. "Your nipples are hard."

"It's cold."

"You're saying when I put my finger in you, you didn't like that?"

"Of course I didn't, Sade! Stop acting like a dense prick, why would I like you doing that against my will? And what happened to not forcing people against their will? Huh?"

She still refused to look at him. "Is it against your will?"

"Am I tied up?" She looked closer toward him with that.

"Yes. But apparently you either like being tied up, or you like me."

She didn't answer him.

"Which do you think it is?"

"Untie me please," she whispered. "I want to leave."

Fascinating. "You say it like we're just playing a little game and you're ready to quit."

"I don't think you're going to hurt me. And I don't think you're going to believe anything I say."

He hated how partially right she likely was. But he wasn't really sure what he wanted to do with her and he wanted to explore that. He liked her. She was a lot of fun in a different way, regardless of her intentions. If he could ensure her long-term company, then getting to the bottom of whatever she was hiding would eventually come. And she was definitely hiding something.

He angled his head at her. "Considering for a moment... that you might be telling the truth. What could I possibly do to ensure that you are *not* the law trying to incriminate me?"

She looked at him, back to a little hopeful. "I don't know, what do you mean?"

"I mean what would you be willing to do, to prove to me you're telling the truth?"

She seemed to brainstorm quickly. "Oh! What about a lie detector test?"

Sade let his gaze slide over her body, making her look away again. He realized two things in that instant. He didn't care so much about the truth as much as he cared about testing her so called good and helpful intentions. Or use them.

And if she was the law in some capacity... what the fuck did he care? Prison inside, prison outside, what was the difference? "What about... a binding contract?"

Her eyes widened. "Yes!" She added a lot of nodding. "Yes of course, I would be so very happy to sign a contract ensuring you that I will never ever do anything to try to hurt you in any way. Ever."

Despite the fact that her dire eagerness was no doubt hinged on desperation to be free, it still roared through him. The sheer possibilities of opening that Pandora's box before him, finalized it. "Done."

"So untie me?"

"I need to draw the contract up first. And then you need to read it. And sign it." He thought about something then. "Playing along with the idea that you're not a cop, contracts aren't really binding when laws are broken."

She gave him a clueless look that made him sure she was likely hiding something personal rather than not. "What about a confidentiality agreement?"

"That's what I mean. That type of contract doesn't exempt you from being required to tell if you know laws are being broken."

"But... I don't know laws are being broken, except right now. Pretty sure this is illegal."

"This would require something I don't ever do."

"Trust?"

"Exactly."

"But you can trust me!" Like out of all this, that should be the easiest thing for him to see.

He stood and gave a huge sigh and presented his back to her. "Fine," he muttered. "I'll do it. I'll trust you."

"Where are you going?"

"Getting paper to draw up our contract."

"I want to help," she said as he went to the desk at the far side of the room.

She wanted to help? Damn. She may be nice but she wasn't entirely stupid, only annoyingly so. He returned with a notepad and pen. "I'm going to name things I want in the contract. Stop me when you have a question or problem."

"Can you…"

He looked at her and decided now was a good time to build on that trust exchange. Bracing for an attempt escape, he released the mechanism holding her right leg and then the left. She merely groaned and pulled her legs closed. He got the knife and cut the ties holding her hands above her head and she immediately covered her breasts with her arms.

He set the knife on a table between both of them. If she were going to make her move, he wanted to give her that opportunity right away. Keeping enough awareness to defend himself if need be, he opened the lower drawer on the table and pulled out one of the sheets and covered her with it.

"Thank you," she muttered, eyeing him.

He stared at her as she held the sheet to her and sidled to the table and retrieved the knife. Sade held his breath as she looked down at the sheet and started to cut it.

"Turn please?"

What the fuck. "Eyes are closed." Mostly.

A few seconds later, "Okay, done. And thank you."

He opened his eyes to find she'd cut a hole in the black sheet and wore it like a poncho. Stranger than strange, she was. "You're welcome." He began writing, continuing with the odd trust demonstration. The danger alone was a turn on. "You agree to not disclose any of my personal or professional business to anybody."

"Yes," she said. "I agree. Unless it's confession."

He looked at her.

"What? Priests are not allowed to tell!"

She was religious? A fanatic? He waited a moment for the turn off and was relieved when it didn't come. "Not even confessional."

"Fine. I guess I will confess to you if I must."

He eyed her. Did she plan on keeping ties with him? "Yes, you can confess to me if you *must*." He wasn't sure why, but he liked that condition.

"Put on there that you agree not to tie me up like this again." Again? So she was planning on hanging around. He hoped he got to be excited about that at some point in his conversation with her.

"I have conditions too! I have feelings, wants, needs, etc.," she said defensively.

"Fine," he said, writing he would not tie her up like that again. He sat there trying to figure out what was off about all of it. The contract. No, more like her eagerness to sign one. He paused then. Had Lester sent her to try and catch him breaking contractual codes again? Sade tapped the pen on the pad, considering. Consequences for that would be worse than prison and Sade was very bad at keeping contracts of any kind when it came to sexually related things. And fucking Lester lusted to take Sade's position as his father's cash cow. If only he knew how much he wished he could. "Anything else you want?"

She sat like a black statue with a head sticking out and big innocent green eyes sparkling with ideas. "Yes, as a matter of fact there is." Sade tensed in anticipation of her answer. Each one was supposed to lead him that much closer to that something he needed to know. But with her... "You agree to… date me for a year."

Chapter Six

Sade's brows shot up with that train wreck. "Come again?"

"Date me for a year," she said firmly.
He stared at her, officially getting something close to pissed with the process. It was progressively baffling. "Define date."

"As in… be my boyfriend. Boy and friend," she clarified. "And no sex."

Sade knew he should keep his cool in this but he couldn't stop his exploding laughter.

"Why is that so funny?" she asked, sounding confused.

Wow, she was... something. But the thought of any fucking body coming to play him, test or not, felt like a direct challenge. And Sade was definitely up for the challenge if it meant he got to play with her.
"Just a friend," he repeated. "For a year?"

"A year."

Sade tried to think of the upper hand or advantage of that. When he drew a blank he said, "What exactly do we do while dating?"

"That means we speak often."

Speak. Precious. "How often?"

"Daily."

The way the answers burst out had him marveling, "Are you making this up as you go?"

"The details yes," she said innocently before getting defensive. "Sorry I didn't have time to come up with a more solid plan for when you drugged and kidnapped me! And molested! Asshole!"

Goddamn she was intoxicating. Her sincerity was as convincing as it was confounding. "Okay, fine. What else. Speak every day but we don't have to see each other every day. No sex. Do I even want to know why?"

"Why what?"

He lifted his shoulders. "Why no sex!"

"Oh my God, do you think that's necessary for dating?" she asked looking disgusted.

"I very much do think fucking in some sense is part of my dating regime, yes."

"Well not ours," she assured with a pointed look.

Sade stared at the paper with wide eyes, trying not to laugh but she was just so damn cute. He focused on asking the right questions that would get him the right answers or close to them. "Fine, no sex." He wrote out the lie extra neatly.

"And you have to agree to let me help you."

Red flags went up and he squinted his eyes at her, feeling like she were a puzzle or picture in a picture. "Help me how?"

She suddenly got that *figure it out as you go* look again. "Sexuality," she pointed at him.

Sade shook his head slowly, back to fucking perplexed, his cock hard as steel. Either they picked a dumbass for the job or she was truly… something else. Not even detective remotely matched now.

"Sexuality. You want to help me with sexuality?"

"Yes. But you have to *agree*."

Sade wasn't sure why she was hung up on the *agree* part rather than the *sexuality*. "I'm putting my fucking name on this contract. Spit, blood, semen, whatever you like."

"Fine," she said.

"Sexuality?" he prompted for specifics.

"Well…"

"Fucking Christ. Dirty dancing lessons? Erotic movie nights? Church? Jacking off while jumping on a pogo stick, counting pennies with old people?"

She covered her mouth and snickered before widening her eyes. "No!" She held up a hand. "Okay. I'm sorry, I'm trying to word it right, I haven't done this before."

"I wish that was a relief to hear." He stared at the pending oxymoron before him. He was suddenly five years old again at the circus, watching that man do his magic. Only there was no such thing, magic was an illusion. A trick. Somewhere behind the awe and wonder was a reality explaining why the impossible beauty wasn't possible. And yet... that memory came with another who did magic like that with him. And he felt it yearning, hungering to see the performance again. Even though the climax would likely bring his own end... he was that five-year-old kid—fucking spellbound.

"I want to help you with... your sexuality."

His sexuality. "You're making my dick hard again."

Her hand shot up. "I don't mean that part."

He lowered his head and shook it, laughing. "Fucking priceless."

"I just mean the whole package."

"And my dick isn't part of that?" He was beginning to realize that *baffled* was likely going to be a regular occurrence with her.

"It is, but that's not... what I want to focus on."

"Ah."

"I want to focus on the emotional and mental, and spiritual aspects of your sexuality." She said this while rolling her hands under the sheet.

Was she a nun? Did she get struck by lightning and sent to set him on the right path? "And what's so wrong with my sexuality?"

Her brows furrowed now. "You're... into sadism. And masochism." Obvious evils. To her.

"So?"

Her confusion grew, like maybe she certainly expected him to see that was wrong or bad. "Sooooo, don't you want to... experience normal sexuality?"

There it was. The name of her magic trick. Only why she was doing it was yet to be discovered. If it weren't that the one performing the trick was the main attraction, he'd find just the sound of *normal sexuality* boring. He shrugged a shoulder, playing along. "Not really. Unless I'm missing something amazing." He regarded her then. "Are you saying you know how to do this... normal sexuality?" The surprise on her face was his disappointing and yet telling answer. "I take that as a no."

"I never said that."

"You didn't need to."

"I do know, I just... don't think I can teach it. *To* you."

Back to the clueless vanilla virgin. Fucking Christ… how much fun could this possibly turn out to be? "So you want to teach me how to experience normal sexuality but you can't teach me."

"I can give you the tools to teach yourself."

He quirked a brow and lip at that. "Sounds like a real blast." He shifted on the stool, not really bothered with that since he was the one in control here, not her. "So after a year of being my friend and teaching me how to teach myself to have normal boring sex, then what?"

She shrugged as though not hearing how ridiculous that was. "Then we can… end the contract?"

He leaned back a little and gave his own innocent suggestion. "Or renegotiate it?"

She agreed with a careless shrug, "Fine with me."

"And I have some stipulations for you as well."

She should have been worried but she wasn't in the least. "Okay, what?"

"You have no other guy friends while we date."

"Not a problem."

His dick hardened again with her agreement even if it might not be legit. He'd find that out. "Also I need a maid and a cook. I'll pay you."

"I have jobs."

"These will pay far better."

She chewed on her cheek, studying him. "I'll have to think about that one. Leave it open."

"No, we finalize this now."

She again thought about it with a deep sigh, eyeing him as though weighing his worth. "Fine, but I have to give two week's notice."

The final test. "And you have to live here."

"Oh absolutely not!" Like he were being ridiculous.

"I have another bedroom, don't worry. No sex, remember?"

Again she angled her head and pursed her lips like she were working her own angles wide open. "How much pay?"

"Two thousand a month."

Sade held his breath as she slid her jaw to the side, staring hard at him, her eyes slits. He somehow got harder than he already was. If she agreed to that, he would nearly cancel out her belonging to another. "Make it four if I live here."

Fuck yes. "Deal." They stared at each other for a few moments and he wondered with a jut of his chin. "What about me and girls?"

"What about you and girls?"

"You okay with me having girls as friends?"

She shrugged and lowered her gaze. "I don't care about that. This isn't that kind of relationship."

He smiled a little. He'd see about that. He certainly would not fucking share her. He was not the sharing type at all and was possessive to the point of psychotic. It's the reason he didn't go around involving himself in *relationships* like this. But she was… just different enough in every way that he found he could make exceptions to his rigid sexual rules. Worst-case scenario, he'd simply break the contract and end it. Maybe by fucking her if his fickle dick should comply.

"Are we done?" he asked.

She looked up at the ceiling a moment then leveled her gaze at him. "One last thing."

"What's that?"

"I need to kick your ass before I sign it."

"Baby," he stood, setting the paper down. Before he could say the words *bring it*, she already brought it with a fucking foot to his chest that sent him stumbling back. By the time he got his balance, she'd peppered his entire front with strikes that would leave nasty marks.

She was so fucking fast in her attack, he only had time to block. He needed her in a corner he quickly realized. Using his stature, he managed to finally get her close enough to one and shoved her into it. With the length of his body pressed hard into hers, he looked down at her turned face, both of them winded.

"You sign our contract with pain?" He gasped several times. "My cock is so hard for you right now. And I don't really like your type."

She grunted but didn't attempt to move.

"You like the way I feel pressed into you? I have a feeling you like a lot of hard things pressed into you."

"I like kicking your ass, that's what I like," she gasped.

"Are you done?"

"Are you still conscious?"

"Never more alive. If you want to beat me unconscious, you'll be here a while."

"I've got a whole year," she said, breathing heavily under him.

"Fuck…" he closed his eyes a moment, "you're like a sadomasochistic dessert. A pretty little cupcake I want to devour in one bite or maybe smell and lick all over before sinking so very slowly into you."

She gave a little growl. "Okay fine, I'm done. You're making this all awkward."

"You're done?"

"As in done kicking your ass. And I'm fucking starving. Whatever was in those drugs has my tongue feeling like I've been licking cotton. They better not have long-term effects, I'll be so pissed at you. I believe in healthy bodies and you just ruined my track record with that shit!"

Sade was back to being confounded with her form of truce. He loved the fascination of her and hated the unpredictability. Which made her irresistible.

"I can order out," he said, while smelling her hair. "Chinese?" She smelled just clean. Like a little girl that bathed without soap maybe. Or scent-free if he had to guess with her *track record* comment.

"You paying?"

Sade felt her body relax and slowly followed suit. "If you make me."

"I'm making you."

"I guess I will then. Since you demanded so nicely."

"I am a *very* nice person," she shoved him and he allowed the force to move him off. His body hummed as he watched her, gliding to the door in her sheet.

Sade stood rooted, fixated. What on earth had he just stepped into with little Miss Mercy? The endless possibilities had him giddy with desire.

"Don't forget the contract," she called as she went. "Where the heck is the actual exit on this demonic den of yours?"

Sade grinned and followed her. "I'll lead the way."

The contract was as good as done. Paper or not. But he'd get to that anyway. To make it official in her mind at least.

Chapter Seven

Mercy stood at a juncture in the rabbit hole. She was no longer looking over her shoulder, keeping an eye on the light of the exit, but instead considering which way would take her to the heart of the splintered soul she found herself in.

Her own past screamed at her, said she couldn't do this without succumbing to those nightmares. Everything Sade did, everything about him made her realize the sad facts about herself. She may have overcome her past mentally, emotionally, spiritually, but she had *not* overcome it physically. His look and touch told her that loud and clear, her body cringed when he looked or touched her in any kind of sexual manner. In her own defense, or maybe to her own fault, she'd not had the opportunity to tell whether or not her past still had power over her body, since she had not dated.

"We'll do this together, Mercy. I've not had a daughter, and you've not had a father. We will learn together and we will overcome the odds together."

Her father's mantra. It saw her through many dark days and yes, it would now be hers. She would help Sade learn new tricks and she would learn how to overcome the physical barriers that would come with. Setting out to help him, she knew it wouldn't be a bed of roses. And like her father, she would see it through.

****

Mercy paced in the condo, hitting redial on her phone for the fiftieth time in the span of two days. She was worried sick. Sade left Saturday morning and it was *Monday* with not one call, not one word. He'd broken the contract already! Which made her think of penalties for breaking contracts. Like proper ass kicking. *"I'll be back in a few."* Those were his last words to her.

A few what? Years?

For the past two days she'd given him the benefit of the doubt to death. She'd prepared. Grocery shopped. Cleaned. Organized. Even made a to-do list of ideas to help him learn normal sexuality. Nothing major, just starting slow. Problem was, a lot of it involved touching. Nothing sexual, just small stuff. Soft stuff. Gentle, accompanied with the right words but still, touching nonetheless and she wasn't sure how that would go over with him. Or her.

Mercy growled when his phone went to voicemail again. In anger, she hit end, then send again as if he might feel the torture of her calling on rapid repeat. She wanted to be sure and have a *big* number when she said how many times she called and *no* answer.

She froze in the middle of the room when he picked up his phone. "Wow, I feel like a superstar." The deep sound of his voice touched her in more ways than she cared to count.

"Sade!" she gasped in relief before letting out her fury, "Sade!"

"I'm sorry baby," he said, his voice a low deep rumble. "Ran into some trouble. I'll be home in a few minutes. You okay?"

Mercy covered her mouth to hold back the sudden sob out of nowhere. She didn't understand why she would cry, she barely knew him but the way he'd just spoken with such concern in his usually hard voice. "I'm just…."

"Hey, hey," he soothed, only making it worse. "I shoulda' called."

"You sound… different," she realized, sniffling back her tears. Like he was slurring.

"You cook anything? I'm starving."

Her stomach flipped at hearing the hunger in him. Seemed multi-dimensional. "I did. Spaghetti. I should have warned you that I have little cooking skills."

He chuckled low. "I love spaghetti."

"Good," she nodded, wiping her eyes. "Good, so you'll be here soon?" she double-checked.

"I'm driving up now."

"Okay, I'll… be here."

She hung up and didn't understand her butterflies. New job nerves. She flew to the bathroom and glanced at her appearance, wiping her eyes. She'd put on a bit of mascara to look more professional, like she cared about this job. She even wore common clothes. As in jeans and a t-shirt, like she were comfortable in her own skin. Normal sexuality came with normal dressing. Yes, she wanted to impress him, as her boss and as a friend. Somebody that cared about him for who he was, not merely his… gorgeous…body and bulging… wallet and… muscles and what not.

She hurried out and looked around at the spotless condo and held her breath when he rang the doorbell. She discreetly ran to open it, immediately gasping. "Oh my God!" He was *beat up* again!

"Got in a little accident," he muttered looking her over with one good eye. "Nice."

"You're beat up!" she cried. "Why Sade!"

"It's my job."

"To get beat up?"

"I fight for a living."

She gasped again, feeling light headed and nauseous. "No no no," she whispered shutting the door and locking it, before following his slow walk into the living room. She grabbed hold of his arm when it looked like he was going to sit.

"Jesus, let me get you some ice!"

"No," he muttered, easing down with a stifled groan.

"What? Why?"

"It's how I do it."

"Well that's stupid! I'll get you some Ibuprofen."

"No," he said again firmly. "Nothing for pain."

"Sade that's ridiculous! Look at you!"

He laid his head back and held out a hand toward her. She took it thinking he wanted to get up, only he pulled her onto the couch. "Sit."

She positioned herself at a friendly distance, leaving a hand space between them. "You look like hell," she whispered, cringing at the eye swollen shut. "I can hardly stand to look."

"Thanks," he muttered, sounding exhausted.

"Have you considered another line of work?"

He let out a small half laugh. "Gotta work for the man for one more year. Then I'm free."

"The man? Your dad?" He nodded. "Free from what? Do you owe him something?"

"Yeah. Everything."

"Oh my God, like what? Money? I have money saved, I can help. You don't need to fight."

"You have money, huh?"

She bit her lip. "Yes. I lied about needing it. I was just saying that to be able to come help you."

"Why?" He barely shook his head. "Never mind." Like he was tired of trying to figure that out or didn't want to make her question it. "But I don't just fight for the money."

She stared at him a moment then realized. "Oh Sade, please…" The words were weak like her stomach just at the idea. "Please don't tell me you do this for the pain."

He took a deep breath and let it out. "Sure."

The empty single word made her want to wrap her arms around him. "Listen to me," she whispered, turning next to him. "There are ways to deal with that."

"I'm handling it. Getting my ass kicked while killing a motherfucker serves both my needs just fine. Two birds with one stone. And it's good fucking money."

"But is it good *for* you?"

"Fuck if I care."

"Well you should!"

"Really? Why?" He turned his head to look at her.

"Because you matter!"

"To fucking who?"

"To…" she almost said her but he'd just say she didn't even know him.

"Yeah. Exactly."

"Listen, I know I don't know you well but you still matter to me."

He laid his head back again. "I matter so you can be like your father. Glad to be your first charity project."

"I'm helping you because I want to."

"And I fight because I want to." He shrugged a little. "We're both meeting needs."

"But should you have that need is the question?" she exclaimed quietly.

"Mercy…. I'm tired."

She sighed and stared at him. "Are you still hungry?" She hissed in pain at the idea of him trying to eat. "I'd have to feed you with a straw."

"I can eat," the words slurred a little. "Yes, I'm hungry."

She laid her hand on his leg. "Stay here, I'll get you a plate. What do you want to drink?"

He slowly turned his head and looked at her with his good eye. "Don't fucking talk to me that way."

She drew back a little. "What way?"

"Like a fucking baby."

She stared at him a moment then shook off the bite of his scold. "I'm just doing what I want to do." She leaned her face toward him. "I like talking nice and I'm not going to stop just because you have a problem with it." She got up and headed to the kitchen. "And if you have a problem with that," she called over her shoulder, "you'll have to learn to deal with it. I'm a nice goddamn person and I won't be an *ass* just because you like that!"

"That's much better," she heard him mumble.

"Shut up, I'm not being mean. I'm being… authoritative and passionate."

"Yes, passionate I can handle. Mushy goo-goo shit, no."

She came back with his plate. "I will be mushy when I damn well feel like it too," she said sweetly. "Now what would you like to drink sweetheart?"

"Very funny." He took the plate. "We got any milk?"

"We do since I shopped." Her stomach turned every time she looked at him. His left brow was split wide open on the edge and held together by a piece of fucking tape. Jesus. She hurried and got it and put it on the coffee table and moved it so he could get to it.

"I'm not in traction, I can reach the table."

"I'm just trying to make it easier."

"Well quit. It's annoying."

She moved the table even closer and eyed him. "You're annoying."

He shook his head. "Did you eat, Mother Theresa?"

"I will." She watched him twirl spaghetti on his fork. "Is it good?"

"Yep."

"No awards huh?"

"E for effort?"

She smacked his shoulder then gasped when he winced. "I'm so sorry," she whined.

"Losing my appetite if you talk like that again."

"Oh my God!" she said, unbelieving. "There is no way that you can hate it that much."

"I can and do." He took a slow bite and chewed.

She let him get a few bites in before she returned to her six-inch position next to him. "Like I said," she reminded, evenly and kindly. "I'm not being an ass just because you're broken."

He stopped chewing suddenly and put his fork on his plate.

She sat forward. "I… I didn't mean anything bad by that."

"I'm tired." He set the plate on the coffee table and slowly got up then headed to the hall leading to his bedroom.

"Shit," she muttered. Was it the *broken* word? Or her persistence? Maybe she should go a little easier on him. Not much easier though, he needed to learn normal. Being nice was normal.

Mercy decided to finish off the few dishes and jumped in alarm when Sade appeared on her left. "What is this?"

She gasped and spun away at finding him naked, holding her post-it note. "You're naked!"

"No sex remember? It shouldn't be a problem," he reminded.

"It's very much a problem! I don't want to see you naked. And that is… a note of encouragement!"

"For what?" he nearly spat.

"Just whatever," she said exasperated, still turned. "We can all stand some encouragement."

He slapped the paper onto the counter, making her jump. "Not me. Don't do that."

When she didn't hear him, she turned to catch a glimpse of his backside as he rounded the corner. At seeing the large bruises on his backside, nausea replaced her flustering.

She shut the water off and stared at her shaking hands. Jesus. She'd never get that snapshot out of her head now. Especially the size of his… stuff. It struck terror in her.

She went to the living room and stood there, debating on what to do next. The condo was spotless and yet she felt like she had done *nothing* but mess everything up. God, tomorrow really needed to go better.

Chapter Eight

Only a week into their contract and Sade lay awake, staring at the ceiling, wanting to touch himself but knowing what would happen if he did. He'd need his fix *now*. And he wanted Mercy to give him that. But he hadn't found a way to ask her and the more he went, the more he was sure she would say no, being dead set against masochism and all. Fuck. Worse than that was that other fucking need, revving up inside him. No doubt in response to this train wreck in his sexual schedule. He could feel it prowling around, wondering if the delay meant it was his turn to play. He didn't want to fucking let it play. The idea of losing himself to any need to the point of not caring where he put his dick was just… *fucking* intolerable.

And all that mush shit she slathered on was not helping. She was like emotional hospice or some shit. He turned over on his side, *almost* regretting his decision to have her there. She was nearly painful, but it was a different kind of torture, and not one that got him off. At all. A week of kindness, smiles, and witty banter. Felt like getting his balls licked and he detested the weakness of it all.

The next morning, Sade woke to the smell of bacon and the roar of his sexual appetite. Good morning Vietnam. Fucking warzone in his body. The fighting that he used to feed his sadism was killing him slowly, right on schedule. And while it satisfied his rage along the way, it always drew out his need to feed his masochism, and feeding that was completely hinged on sex in some manner. A particular kind of sex usually took care of him for a while. And denying himself served his masochistic game only so far. It was a fine line he didn't skirt too close to or his sadism would barge in and take the next dance.

He *needed* to figure out how to get this sweet Mercy to help him.

He might have to play the fucking victim with her to get that.

Sitting through breakfast with Mercy had to be *the* most trying ordeal. She waited on him like an invalid but worse than that was the light in those pretty green eyes and the smile on her angelic face. He wanted to sit there and study it. Figure out the trick behind it, challenge it. Crush it. Then he became entrapped with those lips and began fantasizing strange things. How would they look wrapped around his cock? Open wide in orgasm? Wet with his cum? All of it was a sign that he was way off track. He never put his dick in a woman's mouth. But there was just something sweetly demanding about hers. It begged *Sade, fuck me.*

"Are you feeling okay?" she asked, sounding worried. "You look like you're hurting."

"I am." He raised his eyes to hers. "I need to release."

She narrowed her gaze and lifted her coffee cup. "Like... the bathroom?"

"Like in the basement."

At the mention of the basement, he detected a stiffening in her spine. "You work out down there?"

Just talking about it had him dangerously delirious. "I have an orgasm down there. I don't do it often but when I do, I have to be tied up." He stabbed his last bite of eggs with a fork and eyed her. "And I have to have a woman do it." She appeared half confused, half angry, but he wasn't sure about what. He decided to take the plunge. "I'd like you to do it. Mercy."

Her brows narrowed. "Do what?"

Fuck if she wouldn't make him spell it out.

"I mean if I can, of course I'll help you. Just tell me what to do."

His cock pounded fiercely. "I need you to tie me up and… do and say things." Why was it so fucking hard to say to her? Probably because he knew how she'd react.

Silence reigned before she said quietly, "What do I do?"

"Hurt me."

He saw her head shaking before she whispered, "No, no. I can't. I won't hurt you."

"It's not really painful to me." He looked at her. "I have to have this."

She stared with furrowed brows and pity in her eyes. "You only think you have to have it, but we can find a way to meet your need."

"I have to have it that way," he assured, trying to keep calm. "I've tried other ways, they don't work and if I don't have it, other needs come, needs I don't like to meet."

She gave a small shake of her head, still troubled. "Sade, I won't hurt you, not ever. What other needs?"

He hit his fist on the table making her jump then turned his head right, clenching his eyes tight. "Fine. I'll get somebody else."

"What?" she asked, alarmed.

He looked at her now. "I'll call Tabitha. She'll take care of it."

"No!" Mercy said, standing. "No, you're not calling another woman to do that."

"You have no say over that, remember? Ours isn't that kind of relationship." He aimed a hard stare at her.

She gripped the back of the chair. "That is *not* normal sexuality, Sade. You said you'd let me teach you."

"I'm not stopping you from teaching me. But you can't expect me to learn shit in a few days with sweet words, smiles, and happy eyes. I have a need and it's past time I met it."

"What will happen if you don't? Have you considered self-disciplining?"

"What the *fuck!*" He stood now, shaking his head at her. "I do this twice a fucking year, don't talk to me about self-discipline."

Her mouth remained in that disgusted shock position. "Why a woman?"

"You prefer me use a man?" he asked, annoyed.

Her lips moved with attempted speech but nothing came out, so she paced, shaking her head. "No," she muttered. "This is wrong. I won't be a part of this."

"You don't have to."

She snapped her gaze to him. "Do this and the deal is off. I swear it is. You said you'd let me help teach you normal sexuality and that is *not* normal Sade to have somebody hurt you, some other woman hurt you and what does…" she crimped her face with open disgust, "what does she have to say to you?"

"Not your fucking business."

"Not my business?" she muttered, pacing again before pointing at him. "I'm done here if you do it. I'll leave."

"Fine. Leave. I don't care." Sade shoved the chair down and walked off, pulling his phone from his pocket. He called Tabitha and just like that it was done. Scheduled for that evening. He'd schedule it immediately but he needed to prepare.

"Who was that?" Mercy demanded from behind him.

"My fix." He slid his phone back in his pocket.

Her eyes widened. "Your *fix*. So you just call up a whore and she runs over to fix it for you?"

"Pretty much. And a very well paid whore."

Mercy stood there shaking her head. He was pretty sure she was trembling in anger. Not as much as he was. "Wow," she gasped.

"Yeah, you wow it up. But don't come calling yourself my friend and run away when I really need you just because you don't like my needs."

"I don't like hurting you!" she yelled at him.

"Well that's too fucking bad," he yelled back. "I need to have pain to release, you think I started out wanting it to be that way?" He walked slowly toward her. "You think I *groomed* myself for this? No, baby, that was done by my father and his whores since I was seven." He aimed a finger in her face. "Don't you fucking judge me, you don't know the first thing about me and what I've done to *deal*. Miss *Mercy*."

Sade stormed out of the condo, his confusion and pain disappearing in the wake of his rage. Something he really didn't need anywhere in the vicinity of his sexual dilemma. *Fucking bitch. Fucking friend my ass.*

****

Mercy called Sade's phone when her anger was at boiling. Of course he'd let voicemail get it. "You listen up," she said, pacing. "You bring a woman here for that and I'm gone. Final warning." She hung up and growled. *I'm gone.* What the hell kind of leverage was that? Ah right, he thought she knew something bad on him. She dialed his phone back with trembling fingers and waited for the voicemail. "And also?" She grit her teeth, suddenly worried about using that threat. "I'm not happy about this." She hung up, throwing her phone on her bed. "Not happy about this, good one. Because he gives one iota about what you're happy with."

What exactly was he going to have this woman do? Not her business? Well yes, it kinda was if she wanted to know the extent of his… condition. She froze with the idea and cringed right after. But… how else would she find that out?

She hurried out of the room and to the basement when she was sure the coast was clear. She searched around the scary place and finally spotted something that could work. But dared she?

When doing things that are hard, but necessary, never quit. See it through.

Her father's mantra decided it.

She would hide and learn exactly what it was that Sade had this woman do to him twice a year.

Now, to appear like she'd left and wasn't there. Oh, she knew what to do. Just like he'd done. Hide her car at the parking garage and jog back. Thank you Mr. Sade for that idea.

An hour later, Mercy sat just outside the basement door, listening for the sound of him returning with his well-paid whore. She'd nearly fallen asleep twice before the dreaded sound finally came and sent her bolting up and carefully entering the basement. Hurrying to her hiding place behind the desk, she prayed he didn't need anything from it. Worst-case scenario, he'd find her and… well. He'd find her.

The hope that he'd changed his mind died when he heard mumbling. The door to the basement opened and she heard the lock engage. "Worried about company?" a sultry female voice asked, turning Mercy's stomach.

If he answered her, it wasn't audible.

"You know the drill," she muttered. "Get undressed."

"Yes ma'am." The low rumble of perfect submission made her heart race.

Mercy swallowed at finally seeing him. He stood naked next to that weird round thing on the wall. The one that looked like a human-sized dartboard with the restraints. Dear God would she be able to watch this?

He faced Mercy, blindfolded, and stretched out his arms. Mercy's breath froze at seeing him naked again. So much muscle. Her heart hammered in her chest now. He reminded her of that body in the biology books, the perfect one. Except for his penis. That reminded her of that horse she'd seen in the field when she was nine. She noticed something along his inner thighs, white exact lines. Scars? They looked like marks you make when you take score. Judging by the number of them, the game was nightmarishly long.

Mercy's gut clenched when she finally got a look at the woman. Dressed in all shiny black—pants, top, and high-heel boots. What did she think this was, the Matrix? She approached Sade and guided his arms into the restraints, then secured them, her long ponytail swishing around as she went about her jolly business. Bound at the wrist, elbow, and shoulder, the woman then strapped his legs the same. And wide open. Lord. Mercy's eyes couldn't leave his giant manhood, standing straight out. Her tummy felt weird and tingly at the sight. He was terrifying and maybe… fascinating.

Mercy watched the woman put something around his neck, speeding up the butterflies in her stomach. A chain hung from it all the way to the floor. Mercy fought to see what she did at his groin now. Sade made grunting, straining noises that scared and angered her.

The woman stood and walked to a table nearby and fiddled around, but Mercy didn't look, she was too busy trying to discern the contraption she'd attached to his groin. It wrapped his penis in some kind of harness, covering his scrotum, upper legs and waist. She realized the thing around his neck was now attached to that. Her heart raced at panic speeds imagining what it was for.

Pain.

The idea that he had to do this just to have sexual satisfaction brought a sob in her throat. She bit her lip hard, blinking back burning tears. *"Groomed by my father and his whores since I was seven."*

Jesus.

The woman returned, holding some kind of… holy mother of God she had better not hit him with that. It appeared to be a club bearing long black straps with metal tips.

"Are you ready baby?" she heard the woman ask.

Mercy watched Sade's body heave without answer.

The woman stooped and took hold of that chain leading to the contraption strapped to him then swung that thing in her hand and struck his chest. "I asked you a question, you piece of shit."

Blood trickled from the holes she'd made on his chest and he stifled a groan before growling, "Yes!"

Mercy clamped her hand over her mouth as the woman slowly wrapped that chain around her hand and yanked a little, making him groan hard.

Mercy couldn't tell if it hurt or felt good, she hated this.

"Do it," he rasped, his head turning right. "Fucking do it!" he roared. "Do it to me!"

She yanked the chain hard with a yell and swung the cruel whip. She flicked the chain between yanks and it made his manhood jolt around, bringing another long groan encased in pain. She whipped him and tugged the chain and Mercy realized it was strangling him! His head thrashed and every muscle bulged and strained, but it was the blood the woman drew with her next lashing that launched Mercy from her hiding place.

"Stooooooop!" she screamed.

The woman jerked around as Mercy ran and stood before him, blocking the way. "Who the fuck?"

Mercy turned in panic at hearing him choking still. "Undo him," she screamed, fighting with the hellish ties, "he can't breathe! He can't breathe!"

"I have a job I'm paid very well to do."

"Ta-bitha," Sade barely managed.

She turned to the woman. "Let him go!" she grabbed her and pushed her to Sade. "Untie him!"

She did as told finally. "Who the fuck is this, Sade?"

Sade gasped on air. "Mercy, what the fuck," he said while coughing.

"Tell her to stop," Mercy whispered up to him. "Please. Or I'll make her stop, I will and she will need an ambulance, so help me God." The words barely strained out with her crying.

"You want me to kick her ass?" Tabitha asked him.

"No!" he yelled. "Don't you fucking touch her. Undo me and leave."

"I'll pay her, I promise," Mercy said.

"Fuck you Mercy," Sade muttered.

"I'm sorry," she wailed. "I won't let you do this."

Chapter Nine

Sade finished ripping off the restraints and blindfold in time to see Tabitha get in Mercy's face with her finger, which Mercy broke in a flash before shoving her back.

Tabitha flew at her in a screaming rage and Mercy met her with a foot to the chest and sent her sprawling.

"Tabitha!" Sade yelled. "Leave!"

Gasping for air and clutching her chest, the woman didn't argue. She stumbled her way out of the room and Sade's fury took him by surprise. He stormed over to Mercy and grabbed her by the upper shoulders and shook her.

She only clenched her eyes shut and let out a cry. He wanted her to fight him! Fuck! He shoved her away and paced in useless fury, his sadism clawing at his dick, begging him to use her. Right there in the basement, he could do it. He could let his sadism have her, he so fucking could. Three more seconds and he would have been done if she hadn't interfered!

"Are you happy now *Mercy*? I was *seconds* away from what I'm dying for and you just took it from me!" he yelled. "You call yourself a friend?! Is this your normal sexuality? —Fucking show me how!" He slammed his palms on his bloody chest. "Make my dick come with it Mercy." He snatched his clothes from the table when he felt himself getting to that point of wanting to kill. "Everything but my *dick* in that *treatment.* Thanks *friend!* Who the fuck needs their dick in sexuality? Who needs their dick for fucking, well it doesn't matter with me." He got in her sobbing face now. "Because I can't fuck—I. Can't. *Fuck!* There! Now you heard it. I can't keep my dick hard in the pussy of a woman, are you happy now? Are you going to let me practice on you, Mercy? No, I don't think so, because you lock up when I'm within six inches of you, Miss Normal Sexuality. You wouldn't know normal if it hit you right in your pretty pussy that *drips* down your fucking thighs for me. Just for me!" He grabbed her face in both hands and kissed her with a brutal force. At feeling her perfect mouth turn to eager plump silk, his sadism sky-rocketed, wanting to tear into all of her innocent softness—break her—tear her apart—right then and fucking there.

He stormed to the door and turned to her. "This contract is *over*! You're just another fucking mirage on my road to hell." He pounded his chest with a fist. "This is my pain and misery, and it's *my way!* Not your way! I decide that, I control the pain! Not you! Not anybody, not ever!"

He slammed the door on her begging and lies. He'd not be lured a step further into her game. It was sicker than any he'd ever played and more lethal. Nobody would take his control from him, his way of dealing. No fucking body.

****

Mercy fell to her knees feeling like such a failure. He was so right. She was such a hypocrite with the normal sexuality crap. Oh my God, she didn't realize how desperate he was. She didn't know. She needed to explain that to him, make it right. They could figure out a solution, she just needed to understand more, talk to him.

Mercy hurried out of the basement in time to hear the front door slam shut. "Sade?" She ran to the door and yanked it open. "Sade!" she yelled. "I'm sorry!"

Mercy ran back in and found her phone and called his cell while pacing in the living room. Of course it went to voicemail. "Sade, please come back," she said. "I'm so sorry, I was wrong, you're right. I had no idea how serious it was, I was wrong, please," she strained around a sob. "I'm sorry. I'm sorry, okay?"

The message cut her off and she hung up. He was so furious. She didn't blame him. How embarrassed he must be. And then she hurt that girl. Pretty sure she cracked her chest bone, she didn't hold back, she was scared and furious.

Mercy flew to her room and got her purse and keys. She'd go look for him. Maybe he was going to the club. Running out of the condo, she looked for her Juke. Gone. Did he take it? Why would he? God, the *parking garage.* She ran the few blocks and got in her car and sped through the city, calling his phone every minute and leaving a more calm voicemail while wanting to scream. "Sade, listen. We all have our things, our issues. I want to help you with yours in a way you approve." She went on and on with words that amounted to a broken record then threw the phone onto the seat.

Parking as close as she could to the club this time, Mercy hurried to the place, bringing her phone and leaving her stick. She approached the front, not wanting to deal with that back crowd. A big Saturday night meant a packed crowd.

Getting into the building required her ID, which sent Mercy running back to her car for it, as well as money. By then she had the sense to grab her walking stick before racing back.

Still calling his phone, she left another voice message. "I'm at the Black Velvet looking for you. Please, I need to talk to you." She stuffed her phone in her back pocket and her collapsed walking stick in her bra under her arm. Thankfully she had on her running shoes, she just might need them. It took her thirty damn minutes to get to the front door again, where they finally let her through after telling her they didn't know a Sade. Yeah right.

She entered the club and her survival instincts exploded with the booming music and thick smell of smoke, cologne, and perfume. And one other smell. Body sweat. It raised her hairs more than anything. The smell of bodies grinding in ways that lead to gratuitous and often unsolicited sex, triggered all the wrong instincts in her.

She made her way through the thick crowd, looking for Sade. Looking for anybody that might be in charge in some capacity. She finally spotted a bar and five minutes later, stood behind the wave of people placing orders. She looked around, still unable to see anything but the dense wall of people moving to the thumping airwaves suffocating her. How the hell did they stand it in there?

A murmur of sound gradually rose with the music, loud voices among it. Mercy searched for where it was coming from while a bartender climbed on the bar and peered out into the crowd.

Mercy read his lips. *Fight.*

Shit. Why was she *sure* Sade was in it? Opening her stick, she wove her way through the bodies in the direction the bartender had pointed. She finally made it to the edge of the crowd. "Ah shit," she whispered, seeing Sade in the open square that was officially now a fight rink.

The dude he was fighting was a head taller than him and giving him an ass beating. "Sade!" she screamed from the edge, her voice drowning in the violent hungry chanting.

She pulled out her phone and dialed 911 and reported a deadly fight at the Black Velvet. Mercy's stomach was in knots watching Sade get beat. Then she realized what was going on. He was getting his pain. One way or another.

This was her fault. If she'd just let him finish he wouldn't be getting beat to death now. This was worse. The man clotheslined Sade and slammed him to the floor. Mercy was once again at that threshold where survival instincts kicked in to protect. And in this case, Sade was the victim.

The giant sat on Sade now, delivering blows right to his face. He appeared unconscious and the man was content to beat him till there was no more life in him!

Mercy raced out and struck the man on his fat neck, where it counted the most.

The crowd exploded in shock as the giant jerked an angry glare her way. Ah shit. He had to be on something for that hit not to do more than piss him off. She backed up and glanced around, calculating her options. The man slapped at his neck while approaching with lethal intent and a sneer. Mercy swung the stick in a blur of moves, hoping to confuse him. Seconds later, she planted it hard between his legs, making his eyes pop. He dropped to his knees at the roaring approval of the crowd while the music blasted on. Mercy jabbed the stick into his trachea just as two bodies came at her from the right.

Here we go.

She spun, her fighter's eye seeing dummies with wooden heads, not humans. Using an old-fashioned bat swing, she hit the side of one head and used the momentum to slam her foot into the other. Another body came at her and it got really hairy. Bodies began dropping as she put more power in each strike with lethal aim before they outnumbered her more.

Mercy's head snapped with the sound of breaking glass. Shit, hit from behind. She stumbled and shot the stick over her shoulder, connecting with teeth.

A roar came through the crowd followed by a flying body through the air, slamming the dude that hit her. The circle of bodies all around suddenly widened, letting Sade have at him. Sade's fists rained down fury on the man as the yell of *cops* rang in the air.

Another ran for Sade and Mercy saw the flash of metal in his hand. Her heart faltered and she torpedoed her stick at his arm. The weapon hit the floor and Sade broke free, diving on it then springing up to aim the gun at the guy he'd already half killed.

Shouts erupted around them, "Drop your weapon! Drop your weapon!" Four policemen aimed guns on Sade and Mercy flew to shield him.

"Don't shoot!" she screamed then turned to Sade. "Give me the gun," she gasped,

"before they kill you."

He wiped the dripping blood on his shoulder. "Let them," he said, pushing her aside.

Mercy refused to move as they yelled threats to shoot if he didn't comply now.

"Please," Mercy shrieked. "I'm sorry, I'll do what you need me to! Put the gun down!"

"It ends tonight, it ends right now," he roared at her, trying to push her aside.

He was going to get himself killed. Mercy eyed the gun and obeyed the instant weapon disarming reflexes she'd mastered. Two seconds later, she was sliding the gun onto the floor toward the police.

At the rush of policemen, he fell to his knees, hands behind his head, with eyes on her. So full of... hate. They wrestled him to the floor and Mercy ran forward. "It's not him! I'm the one that called, he didn't have the gun I knocked it out of a guy's hand and he picked it up. He was just protecting me!"

"Follow us to the police station for questioning," the one kneeling on Sade's back yelled.

"Yes sir, yes sir," Mercy whispered before following out behind Sade and the other cops. They let her drive herself to the police station and she went in and gave her story. After reading her statement, the policeman sighed and left with it. Nearly an hour later, they brought Sade to her and released him. They didn't have anything to keep him on. But Mercy was sure they did, only chose not to.

Once in her car, they drove in silence all the way back to the condo. The tension in the air was hard to breathe in and while she didn't want to make it worse, she had to say something. She went back and forth between nice and firm. She was still very sorry but didn't want to be mushy about it. Fine line.

"I'll renegotiate the contract. To include physical."

No answer.

Mercy waited in torment. "I'm really sorry, Sade." She kept her tone firm, not mushy.

Still no answer. No answer until they got back and he opened the door. "It's all gonna work out. I wanna thank you for having my back. Nobody's ever done that. Not for free. I hope you enjoyed the ride." He glanced at her for several seconds. "Because your illusion of control is over."

She stared at him as he slowly got out of the car, her stomach in knots. She didn't like his tone. It sounded too calm.

Chapter Ten

Mercy followed Sade up to the condo, staying close in case he needed anything. Like another human to fall into. She hurried ahead and opened the door for him and without a word he went in and walked toward his room.

"Are you hungry? Thirsty? I have leftover meatloaf."

Still nothing. She closed her eyes, ready to collapse in relief. He was home at least. Safe. Please God, help me out here. Help me know what this man needs, give me the strength to help him.

She saw blood on her hands and frowned. Was it hers? His? Somebody else's? She went to her room and grabbed clean clothes then headed to the spare bathroom to take a shower. Before she did, she checked on Sade and found the light in his bathroom on and the door shut. Good. He needed a shower.

The idea of showering with all those wounds on him, made her cringe though. Mercy got in the shower and began going over what she could do different. She had to concede that helping change his sexuality couldn't be done without engaging his... sexual parts. How foolish to even try. Especially with him and his needs. Live and learn. Mercy rinsed her hair and lathered up her body next. She'd have to break down and incorporate physical. Somehow. She shuddered at the thought as she rinsed.

The sound of a horn reached her and she turned off the water, listening. She thought about it then. Not a horn, more like... a trumpet sound? What the hell?

Getting out the shower, she crept to the door and opened it, listening. Nothing. But her body was humming with fear for some reason. She dressed quickly and quietly exited the bathroom and made her way into the living room. Looking around, she found it empty. She scoped out the dining room and kitchen and found everything in order.

Double-checking the locks, she went back to her room and regarded the light in Sade's bathroom. Walking over, she knocked on the door. "You okay?"

Not getting an answer, she knocked harder. "Sade?"

The water was running. Panic slammed her and she tried to open the door. She banged loudly. "Sade!" she screamed.

Shaking, she darted back about five feet and shot to the door, slamming her body into it. It banged open and she fell into the bathroom in a sprawl. "Sade!" she screamed, scrambling to her knees and crawling to the tub.

"Sade please!" She pulled his arm up and found a long horizontal slit oozing with blood. "Oh God," she choked, holding the limb like a bat and squeezing with all her might to stop the flow of blood. His eyes were shut and his mouth slack. She needed to check his pulse but she didn't want to let go. "Sade, wake up!" she yelled through a sob.

The first aid kit in the basement flashed in her mind and she reluctantly ran for it. Sprinting back to his bathroom, the kit flew open and contents exploded everywhere. She crawled on the floor and grabbed the rubber tourniquet and raced to the tub, tying it above his elbow. She then scrambled for the gauze. "You're okay," she whispered, shakily, wrapping his arm. "I got you. Gonna wrap this up," she barely managed as she wound it tight then held it in both her hands again. "Gonna stop this bleeding," she sniffed, calming her tone. "Not a problem. I'm a nurse." Tears surged with a sob. "I got your back," she choked. "But you gotta stay with me, stay with me. Sade, can you hear me? Don't leave Sade," she said loudly. "Not yet, it's not your time."

When the wound finally stopped bleeding, she quickly felt his pulse and wailed in relief at the faint sensation still there. She let the water out of the tub next. "My daddy used to say," she began softly, "that some people are born to survive. No matter what comes their way, no matter how much pain is dealt them, they live. They survive it somehow. That was me, he said. And I think it's you too?" She nodded, petting his face. "Why else am I here, right? I'm supposed to be here!" she cried.

Mercy needed to get him to his bed. God how? He was dead weight. She needed help.

Mercy found his phone and searched the contacts. "Bo," she gasped, remembering that name. She hit send and when he answered, she sobbed out all the details. He was coming right away. He wouldn't tell anybody, she'd made sure. Sade wouldn't want people knowing this.

When Bo got there, he helped move him to the bed. He was so tore up over the sight of him, crying like a baby, making Mercy cry too.

"He's a good guy," he kept saying. "He just had a hard life. That's all. He takes care of me, did you know? He don't really hurt nobody that don't deserve it." He shook his head, looking confused. "I don't get why now, he didn't even have a sexorcism."

"A what?" Mercy said, confused. She pulled Bo out of the room and into the hall. "A what?"

Bo looked suddenly worried to tell. "He doesn't do it often," he whispered. "But when things get too bad, he has to get with a lot of women… you know?"

Mercy covered her mouth. No, she did not know, and she didn't want to in that second. She patted Bo on the shoulder and he nodded then went back and sat in the chair next to the bed like he planned to watch over him.

Mercy was glad for it. She walked over and touched his arm and whispered, "I need to go to the pharmacy for supplies. Can you stay with him until I get back?"

He gave her a confused look then nodded.

"I'm a nurse. I know what to get, okay? You need anything?"

He shook his head, looking back at Sade. "I'm good. Just hurry and get what he needs." He looked at her. "He'll be fine."

It was a statement that needed confirmation and Mercy nodded. "I'll have him good as new in two days." She patted him and hurried off.

Coming back with all the supplies she could think of, Mercy checked his blood pressure and let out a sigh of relief at finding it not as bad as before.

When she was sure he was stable, she dismissed Bo and went take a shower, leaving the door open so she could hear. The deal was, nobody was to know about this and Bo agreed. She hoped he kept his word.

When she was done doing everything she could think of, Mercy sat on the edge of Sade's bed and watched him. She stared at him in sleep and scooted closer to see him better. She wondered if he ever took out the silver studs on his brow and if they bothered him. She regarded the ring on his right nipple next and wondered why just the right one. Reaching up, she felt his forehead and found it warm but no fever. She turned his arm and made sure his wound wasn't bleeding. Another sigh of relief to find it wasn't. She stroked his arm softly, wanting to take away his pain, wanting to know how to do that.

He suddenly mumbled something and her heart lurched as she leaned in to hear. "Shhh, you're ok. You're going to be fine." She stroked the side of his face and his head lolled toward her.

"W-…" A few seconds later, he seemed to fall back asleep. Mercy was drawn to study his face up close, particularly his full lips and the gash across the top right edge. They were fuller when at rest. Soft even. Such a contradiction to everything else about him. She realized his lashes were rather long. She hadn't noticed. Maybe because she could never get past those bright gray eyes?

"Mercy," he mumbled.

Her eyes flew up to his and found them still closed, his brows drawn together. "I'm here," she whispered.

"You're here," he whispered back. "Always here. Here to stop me," he barely managed. "Next time…" he slowly smiled. "I'll make sure."

"Okay, you'll make sure."

He barely nodded. "You won't stop me."

Panic slammed her guts and she withdrew from him a little. Dear God. "Why?" she asked, her whisper hoarse. "Why are you doing this?"

"Because… I can."

An odd anger burned through her at his words. Because he could. There wasn't much he could do growing up. But now he could, couldn't he? And yet. Why was she here? In his life? Why did she find that envelope that day? Accident? Fate? What was her purpose? Wasn't it to help him? Why was everything backfiring?

A memory surfaced in her mind. Not long after her father had rescued her. She'd wanted to die too, but oh, he'd not hear of it. He stood in the way of her pain and her death and he insisted she live. And she did.

She had to be stronger than his pain. She wouldn't let him die. She'd make him live. She'd make him overcome. She'd teach him how to survive no matter what it took. Just like her father had done with her.

Chapter Eleven

Sade woke up and realized he couldn't turn. He opened his eyes and gazed around. In his room. He looked right and narrowed his gaze in confusion. Why was he tied to the fucking bed? He moved his legs and found they were tied too. What—the fuck?

He yanked on the restraints and found them solid. "Mercy!" he yelled.

A few moments brought her running to the door with clothes in her arms. "You're awake," she sang, all sunshine and smiles.

"Why am I tied?"

She walked into the room and widened her eyes at him. "Because you're a threat to my work."

"Your work?"

"Yes. My helping you. I can't help a dead man. And you seem hell bent on being that."

"Un. Fucking. Tie me."

She dumped the armful of clothes on the bed. "No can do."

"Mercy."

She folded the clothes, not looking at him. "Yes?"

"I'm going to get untied from here," he began, "and when I do, I'll put you where I am. Are you sure you want to do that?"

She shrugged. "Taking my chances. But I'm pretty good at restraining. Had plenty of training in that."

"That a fact," he said.

"It very much is." Her words were sincere and light as she put clothes in his drawer.

In that second, his sadism roared to life and pulsed hard in his cock. Not fucking surprised. She'd done it now, hadn't she? Is this what she wanted? To be a target of his sexual sadism? Well it was too late now, he knew how it went. That hunger wouldn't rest until it had what it craved. And now it craved Mercy. Her broken beneath him.

He was suddenly very fucking glad he was tied. For now.

"I'm hungry," he said, ready to escape while he wasn't too pissed. Getting too pissed made it that much harder for him. He just needed to find her weakness and use it. Just a matter of time. A day maybe.

She brightened. "I made scrambled eggs and bacon. Would you like toast with that?"

"The works. And milk."

"Coming right up." She headed out.

"And I need the bathroom." Fucking ought to be interesting.

"Coming with your toilet."

His toilet. What the fuck.

She returned with a tray and he spied an empty mason jar. "I'm not pissing in that."

"You'll go on yourself then. And if you do that, I'll let you sit in it a while before I rectify that foolish decision."

Sade pulled carefully on the restraints, pissed they were still just as uncompromising as when he first began working them. It was the fucking *way* she'd tied it, and with what she'd tied him. His entire forearms were harnessed—no doubt to protect his wound. And it was anchored to a kind of swivel base so that he could move it around all he wanted. Like rattling a cage, but that's all it did because that's all it was designed to do.

He let her feed him, all the while staring at her.

"You know, once I tried to kill myself." She flashed him a scar on her right arm. "Was like deja-vu when I found you. I never considered what my dad had felt during that. I was only thirteen and it had to be hard."

Sade slowed his chewing, wanting to know all about it but not ready to ask.

"It was such a bad time." She presented him with another bite, her gaze on his mouth. "Only like a year after he'd came and kidnapped me from where I was staying."

Sade was no longer hungry for food. He wanted to stare and contemplate her. He shook his head and she set the fork back on the plate.

She gazed blankly into the air, her mouth very different looking without a smile. He remembered again how her lips felt under his brutal kiss and his dick got harder. He wanted to do things to her. And if she somehow found herself in the path of his sadistic desires it would be different with her than it was with the paid whores. He felt it burning in him. The near insatiable appetite he'd have with her. Never getting enough. She would break in the first hour he was sure.

"Those nightmares wouldn't stop," she continued, lowering her head for a moment. "Dad would be there every night, wrap me in his arms and tell me it was all over but…" her head shook slowly, "…it wasn't over. It was alive. Inside me. The fear, the pain, it was… so real." She moved the food around on the plate now. "He didn't save me from that life once. He saved me a million times. As many times as I needed saving."

Her tone said this was the method she would adopt with him. And Sade found it difficult to be all that pissed with her about it. He listened, hoping she divulged more details. That was the other hunger he had with her. To know her intricately, in every way. And exploit it.

"And then I decided I'd make it stop." She presented him with another bite, forgetting he wasn't hungry. But he leaned and took it slowly. "There was only one way to make it all really go away. So I did it. Obviously I wasn't that great at it."

"Obviously," he said, his tone softer, burning to know what would make her go to that extreme.

"But while I was dying, I had this… epiphany," she smiled, looking into the air before her as though seeing it again. "I was so free, I was out of my body, flying around. And then I realized… I was an angel." She aimed incredulous green eyes at him that made his heart beat faster. "And there was this other angel there, and he pointed down and I looked. And I saw me lying there on the floor and my father screaming and crying." The agony in her angelic face for somebody else while she was dying… utterly fascinating. "And… I was so, so, sad for him. And I just knew that… I had to go back. To take away his pain. Anything to take away his pain. Even if it meant facing the nightmares, I would just have to do it." She wiped tears from her face and finally angled her bright green gaze at him, making Sade lower his. He suddenly didn't want to see the raw purity there. Just felt… wrong. The blasphemous kind of wrong.

"I really need the bathroom."

"Oh!" she reached and wagged the empty jar at him.

Sade eyed it, then her. "You plan on helping with that?"

She bit her lower lip, thinking. "I better. I don't trust you not to be stupid."

"Smart girl." His dick twitched at the idea of her touch and what it would feel like. The big question was would he like it while not in a frenzy of sadism? The excitement in his body said he wanted to like it.

"I am a nurse," she reminded more herself than him. "I've seen my fair share of genitals."

"Have you," he muttered, liking that she did a bad job of hiding her frayed nerves on that front. "Then why are you nervous?"

"Well, this isn't exactly your typical medical condition." Honesty as usual. His body had a positive response to it. She pulled the covers down over his naked groin and raging erection that she seemed to deliberately not notice. His cock laid thick on his abs, waiting.

"Better hurry."

"Coming." The singsong word came breathy and Sade grunted when she took hold of his dick between two fingers and placed it inside the jar. "Aaand go."

Of course Sade's body refused to cooperate. He knew why too. He wanted to have a fucking orgasm, not take a piss. And once he was done pissing, this would be over. He didn't want it to end and his body didn't want it to end. "It's not coming."

"We can wait a few seconds," she said with ease.

"I hold my balls when I piss."

"Oh. Hm." She looked around and grabbed his empty milk cup and placed it between his legs and barely pushed on his balls.

Sade's dry laughter boomed out.

"What? I'm not touching them with my hand. For this."

For this! His cock jumped in the jar at that little surprise promise. Or was it a slip? Had she meant to say it? It was just as good as a promise coming from her and he'd hold her to it. A charity hand job? Is that what she was thinking of doing? He was desperate enough to not care why she did it, just so she did.

He'd let her play her mercy games with him for a while and see where they took him. If he liked it, he'd play. If not, he'd make his move. She'd earned a little gold star for effort even if he didn't agree with her noble stupid cause. And maybe she'd earned a little respect. Maybe. That verdict was still out and she could surely lose it at any time.

He finally managed to piss.

"Oh," she said in alarm as the jar got really full. "Wow, you were at maximum capacity."

He gave a low grunt and tilted his hips making his cock rub against the container. "Fuck," he whispered, laying his head back.

"What? Does it hurt?" She carefully screwed the lid on the jar.

"Yes it fucking hurts. I need to…" he couldn't bring himself to even say it. Pissed him off that she would have that kind of power over him.

"Okay," she said quietly, setting the golden juice on the breakfast tray and hurrying off like she was afraid to hear it. Oh he was sure she was. Anything to do with sex turned her into a skittish lamb.

For the first three days, Sade played the perfect patient. Mercy played the perfect nurse. On the fourth day of her nursing, his dick was ready to implode. She'd done her healing therapy with him—soft touching… sweet words of encouragement. He wasn't sure what he needed more, to have a raging orgasm or vomit.

He was sure that he was done. And he had his plan in line. Break out and put her right where he was. Play doctor on her like she did on him. She could sure use some sexual therapy. Sade new it was foolish to try and yet also knew he would. Having her tied up knowing his sadism had its sights on her was dangerous.

It came on the fourth day, his answer to that wicked prayer. "I need you to make a phone call for me," he said.

"Oh?" she asked, removing the breakfast tray.

"I need Tabitha to come over. For thirty minutes. In this room. And I need privacy."

She stared at him while holding the tray. Amazing how her brows furrowed with a look of pure confusion. But that other thing was there he was looking for. A spark of jealousy. The idea that she was jealous had presented itself a few times and he wasn't sure how to feel about it. Right then, he knew. He felt impossibly aroused with it.

"I need to fucking release. She's good at hand jobs," Sade lied, eyeing her, waiting for that impossible verdict.

"That won't be necessary," she said, turning.

"Why not," he demanded.

She turned at the door. "Tonight, I will help you with that."

Before he could respond, she walked out. Fuck yes. "Just how do you plan to do that?" he yelled to her.

"I'm sure it can't be that complicated," she called back.

He let his head fall back, his cock ready to burst. She returned with folded clothes a few minutes later. "Tabitha has training in that," he went on, liking the conversation.

"Oh well, you'll have to make do."

"Just call her."

"No," she said, slamming a drawer shut.

"Why not?" He fucking wanted to hear her say it.

"Just don't need her."

"Is that a fact," he muttered.

"Yes sirreee. You need anything before I go? I'm going to the grocery store for a few items. Making lasagna."

He was sure her hand job wouldn't cut it but the raging heat in his cock begged to differ.

"So tonight."

She nodded slowly, keeping her gaze somewhere above his head. "Yep."

"Good," he nearly growled. He was still very hungry to make her pay. His escape plan and his intentions after he did, remained. Make Mercy beg.

While she was gone, he lay there thinking and the first day of incarceration in his own room coming to mind. He'd asked her, "What if I need the real bathroom? You know, to take a shit? I'm not doing it in a jar."

Oh she had that figured out. A long chain to the bathroom. Several times he'd been tempted to wrap it around her neck and make her undo him. But he was pretty sure she wouldn't and he'd end up having to hurt her. He didn't want to hurt her, not like that.

He had other pains in mind, the kind that involved humiliation. Torment. Agony. The sexual kind. His fantasies fueled his patience until they had him so hot, he was ready to burn his chains off.

He remembered her *chatting* thing she did. "I was thinking we could talk after my chores. You know. Chit-chat."

"About what," he'd said.

She'd given a narrowed gaze with a smile. "Stuff. Just regular stuff. Life. Work. Whatever."

"Sex?" he'd said, to the reddening of her cheeks. Amazing that she didn't see how absurd it was of her to try and teach him normal sexuality while she was fucking frigid. Just confirmed that he needed to teach her. He may not know normal sexuality but what he did know, he knew very well.

And during all this therapy, she wore her "normal" clothes. Jeans. And her fucking ass was small and tight, like her tits. He growled and laid his head back, rolling his hips. The covers stroked the sensitive head and he was ready to try and use the friction to orgasm.

No. He'd wait. Wait for her fucking hands on him. The dense heat that filled his groin ranked up there with his bi-yearly sadomasochistic flings he treated himself to.

Maybe an hour later, she came back in with a bottle of water and a straw. "Thirsty?"

"No."

"Do you need anything?"

"Nothing you can give."

"How will you know if you don't ask?"

"Okay," he said, angling his head at her. "I'd like for you to suck my dick just to see if I'd get off, since I don't normally. And I've been wondering what your ass would look like while sitting on my cock. You have a nice tight ass."

"Sade!" she gasped, acting all shocked. "Oh my God, you know I didn't mean that!"

He eyed the pretty pink in her cheeks. "I know you did mean that and you're pretending like you didn't. You know where my mind is and you begged me to tell you so I'm concluding you definitely want to hear it. And you definitely want it."

She sat on the bed and Sade couldn't help but be impressed that she managed nonchalance. "I'd like to try some new things with you."

Lord, here she goes with the Mother Theresa exercises. He could hardly wait.

"I'm going to sit on your stomach for this."

His air left him in shock at that announcement. He waited in silence for the rest of the details. "Oh you're doing this now?" he realized, as she climbed on him.

"It won't take but a moment. Tell me if I hurt you."

"Hurt me. How funny, angel."

He pulled instinctively on the restraints when she placed her hands on his chest, wanting to help with that. His sadism boiled and he gave a hungry grunt at feeling her on him. She was so light. She'd be easy to maneuver in whatever way he wanted. He stared at her waist, sure his hands would encompass the entire thing.

"Okay," she said. "This is a game called *look into my soul*."

He slowly raised his gaze up to hers.

"I'm serious," she whined lightly. "Can you try to be for real? Please?"

"Well since you asked so nicely, and kindness is my weakness," he said dryly.

She sat back a little. "I'm not going to make you do this. You have to agree."

He scanned her body and angled his head, loving how she looked right there. "Do it." He raised his gaze to hers. "Look into my soul. But you may not like what you see."

She gave him a smile that made his heart pound. She was full of strange little tricks and powers like that. He couldn't deny the anticipation either, to see just how much power she had over him, with him.

"Okay, I'm going to hold your face." She placed both hands softly on either side of his face and he struggled not to turn into the touch for a better feel. Then she leaned in.

At six inches away, he smiled. "I could head butt you."

Her eyes widened. "Please, don't do that. It would ruin the entire experiment."

He stared into her eyes. "I'm sure it would."

"Me too," she whispered, no longer smiling while staring back into his gaze.

"What are you seeing, Mercy?"

"I'm seeing..." she began softly with the slightest hint of a smile, "a beautiful man."

Sade bit his tongue, not allowing himself to interrupt her cute little show.

"He's very kind. And gentle. And good."

Sade jerked his head right and laughed.

"What! I'm seeing this, I'm not lying."

He laughed more at the ridiculous lie and she groaned in frustration. He finally turned back to her, worried she'd stop. "Okay, hurry and finish."

"Tell me what you see now," she whispered, holding his face again.

"That's easy," he muttered, going sober as he locked his gaze onto hers for several seconds. "I see a little girl that is playing a naughty game with a very bad man because secretly she wants him to make her scream in…" he angled his head. "Pleasure."

She poked her lower lip in a pout. "I thought sure you'd say angel."

"An angel that ties men up in their own homes, right. Or an angel that comes at night and rubs my cock." He enjoyed the reddening of her cheeks, it was like clockwork. "Points for not breaking eye contact."

"Yes!" she exclaimed quietly, taking the praise. "That was hard."

"Not as hard as my fucking cock right now. Could you slide a little lower?"

She closed her eyes this time.

"Ohhhh," he said, "you dropped the ball and shattered my soul. Thanks."

She busted out in snickers and laid her head on his chest then popped back up. "Sorry, you're right. I seem to suck at this when talking about certain things."

"Sex. When talking about sex. Say it. Look into my eyes and say it."

She met his challenge. "I... have trouble talking about sex when... looking into your eyes."

"Goooood job," he said, impressed. "Wonder if you could do that while I'm fingering your tight, wet pussy?"

That earned her moan of disgust and dismount.

"Done already? What's for dinner?"

She stood next to the bed and gave a light sigh. "Meatloaf and mashed potatoes with green beans and bacon."

He returned his gaze to hers at hearing she wasn't holding it against him. "Is that what I smell?"

An offended gasp escaped her pretty lips. "Why are you looking disgusted? I YouTube!"

"Look into my eyes Mercy."

She cocked her hip and glared at him.

"YouTube is for wannabes."

She gave a tight little smile. "Then I qualify."

He stared at her mouth. "You have a fucking pretty mouth, you know that?" He raised his gaze up to hers, seeing what that did.

"So do you," she said, holding her ground then raising her brows.

He gave her a half smile. "You have pretty tits too." She shut her eyes and growled with a stomp of her foot and he hissed in pain. "Shattered my soul again."

"You already gave your opinion of them." Hurt accusation came with her pointed stare. "No lying when soul connecting."

"Soul connecting. Right." He bit back a smile, finding that so damn stupid and adorable. "And I'm not lying."

She raised her brows. "How am I supposed to know?"

"I lied then," he muttered, staring hard into her eyes. "But not now. You have… *very*… pretty tits. And I don't usually even like looking at them. But yours… I find myself wanting to do so many things with them."

Again she closed her eyes and whined. "Dammit," she hissed. "Lying or not, I can't do it."

"Why so down?"

"Because I'm supposed to be able to do the things I'm teaching you. I suck worse than you!"

"Hey, don't include me in your misguided diagnosis. I never thought I was bad, you did."

She walked back and sat on the bed, facing him. "So, I have a proposition for you."

"My cock is listening."

She rolled her eyes, cheeks turning pink before she plowed on. "We can read to each other. That helps build emotional intimacy I've heard."

"YouTube?"

"No, my psych books."

"Great." He regarded her then, deliberately not touching the part of her willing to build this emotional intimacy with him. "You studying to be a shrink or what?"

"No," she waved a dismissive hand. "Just part of my studies in the medical field. And I think you need to do the things that most people do growing up, that help them connect to the feelings that are… mostly absent in…"

"Go on. Name it."

"People with…"

"Sadomasochistic personalities?" he helped. "See, you're the only one with a problem with embracing it. I know what I am. I accept that."

"I just don't want to offend you," she countered in innocence. "I accept who you are too and I'm not a stranger to the symptoms you have."

"Oh?" How very intriguing. "Do tell. Show and tell even. I hear that's a good form of expression as well. Showing me what you mean?"

"I know what you're doing," she wagged a finger at him. "Not stupid here."

"Mmmm, and that is a fucking turn on to me."

She raised her brows. "Good!"

"Is it? You like me being turned on by you?"

"I like you being turned on by intelligence," she corrected.

"So you're okay if I'm turned on with any woman's intelligence."

"Yes."

"Because Tabitha is pretty smart."

"Oh please!" she snapped.

"She is. And she's very good at making my cock come. Do you know how hard that is to do?"

"She's good at getting kicked in the chest."

Sade had to laugh at that one. "Damn, you are so…" He shook his head trying to decide. "Alluring. Without even trying. Now, look in my eyes and tell me I can like any intelligent woman," he challenged.

She aimed her gaze right at him but then her cocky expression slowly dissolved until she looked at her lap. "Fine, not just any woman."

Sade's heart beat odd in his chest. "Just women like you?"

More hesitancy. She looked completely away from him now and muttered, "Okay fine. One woman at a time." She glanced back at him. So brave. "You are free to like who you want of course but one at a time if you don't mind."

"I'll try my best, teacher. To like just you. For now."

She faced him again, back to eager and moving on. "So what kind of book would you like me to read to you?"

He'd never had so much fun while being tied up and not fucking. "You have any Playboy mags?" At her eye roll, he laughed. "Okay fine. How about erotic horror." The sick look she gave was priceless. "You asked. And it will probably do you some good."

"Me?"

"You need to work on your sexual edge. Sex is a main component in your field of work, doc. You need to be comfy with talking about all aspects of it. Don't you think?"

"You're right." She gave slow firm nods then popped her gaze to him. "Full of self-serving-shit, but you do have a valid point."

He couldn't resist laughing at that. "Busted."

"So, I'll… find some yummy fun, erotic horror reads to go with your dinner."

"I want to shower," he reminded her.

"Bo is coming to help with that. You're not going to be mean to him again."

He shrugged. "Can't make any promises." But in all honesty, despite all the odd fun she was, he was not one to be forced to do anything non-sexual. And he was officially out of patience. And except for her little surprise gift, he was ready to change the game.

Chapter Twelve

Mercy was trying to get why she'd be ecstatic. She had too many things to be nervous about to be that. Like her sexual charity work looming in the next few hours. Yes she was nervous about that but not for the reasons she'd imagined. She was worried she wasn't going to be able to help him. She wanted to Google it but didn't want to set off the wrong triggers. She felt like she was walking a tight rope where that was concerned and needed to take baby steps and not look down or to the left or right.

She'd fed him dinner which was... an erotic experience all by itself. He never said a word, nor did she. He did that gaze locking with her, without being asked, and she'd silently participated. It was a kinky communication of food. And the act of feeding him and nourishing him had a good effect, she was sure. And she liked it. Plus, somewhere behind that hard gray stare he kept trained on her there was something similar to... pleasure of some kind.

Now, she waited for Bo while she saved food and cleaned up. He reluctantly agreed to help him to the bathroom again. She'd used some of her handy-man skills her father had blessed her with and installed an eye bolt next to the toilet. She attached a thick chain to it that led to the bed attachment. Thankfully his bed seemed to be carved out of a massive hard oak. Even if he could dismantle it, he wouldn't get through the door and even if he did that, he wouldn't get very far.

The doorbell finally rang and she hurried to it. Bo stood in the hallway, looking like a centerfold for a clothing magazine. He had those classic perfect features with a pretty body to match. Not all muscle like Sade, but more sleek. He dressed the part too albeit she guessed accidentally. Something about him said he didn't mean to look so good. But right now, he looked like she'd called him in for an exorcism that would end in his death.

"Thank you so much for coming," she whispered, shutting the door behind him and locking it. "How's it going? Any questions asked?"

He looked around as though making sure it was safe before regarding her with a head shake and a, "Nah. Only his close friends and this isn't the first time, if you know what I mean?"

She nodded, gathering as much from his initial expressions when arriving that horrible night. "I already let him know you were coming."

"What'd he say?" His terror was palpable.

"He's fine with it."

"Until he's killing me," he muttered. "Sade don't usually tell what he's really feeling," he barely whispered. "You only know it when you're dying."

She put her hands in her back pockets and attempted a reassuring smile. "He's chained," she reminded him.

Bo's eyes popped. "Death by asphyxiation. My favorite."

"He's fine. For now at least," she said, leading the way then holding up a hand for him to hang back in the hall. "Bo's here," she said to Sade.

"Nice," he muttered.

Mercy went to the bathroom and dragged the large chain she'd put in there, back to the bedroom. She unscrewed the mechanism that would allow her to attach it to the bed, ignoring his stare. "Remember why I had to do this," she muttered.

"Oh, I do."

She sighed and shook her head, avoiding his gaze. "It's more for me, really. I'm nervous."

"Nervous of what?" he sounded disgusted.

"Of you hurting yourself again."

He cocked his jaw slowly, his eyes boring into hers. "Right," he said, his tone indicating it was anything but.

"Stop doing this right now."

"Me. You're the one rattling on."

She eyed him and switched his restraints then released him from the bed.

"Hey Bo!" he yelled.

"Yeah man," Bo hurried to the door.

"What the fuck are you doing here?"

"Sade," Mercy scolded in a hiss. "Don't torment him, he's already feeling bad enough."

"I'm going to kick your ass for helping her imprison me, I hope you know."

Bo nodded with a serious face, his hands in his front pockets. "Yep."

Sade laughed. "But you still gonna do it my brother?" Sade stood now, his towering frame along with the clink of chain and deep voice officially scary now. Bo backed out of the room and into the hallway and Mercy put her hand in Sade's. He snapped his gaze down to her and she met it unflinchingly while holding her breath.

"Just to make sure you don't fall," she said.

"Because you would break my fall, right?"

"I'd try, yes."

He held her gaze for several moments, seeming pissed. "Bo," he called. "You ever met a woman like this one?"

Bo poked his head in the doorway. "Nah man. Not sure who I'm scared of more, her or you."

This tickled Sade's funny bone and he just laughed and laughed. "She's a stick of dynamite?"

"TNT," he said.

Sade regarded her again then muttered for only her ears. "She's fucking crazy is what she is. I'm going to have a lot of fun with her."

Mercy let out a breath when he headed to the bathroom with no more fight. Once the men were in, she announced, "I'll be finishing laundry. Watch your wound and don't open it. I'll dress it again after."

"Oh you can be sure I'm not going to open it and jeopardize our date tonight."

Lord, right. That. Only a few hours away. And what exactly did she have planned for that? She needed to make it count, whatever it was. Needed to be much more than a hand job, it needed to impact him in many ways on many levels. It needed to be a… *heart and soul* job. Good God, corny much?

She thought about doing it in the dark. But was that beneficial to him? God, she was such a hypocrite. No, the dark idea was all for *her*. How pathetic. She needed to decide what she was going to do and just do it. Do what was best for him.

****

Sade wondered if she'd chickened out when she finally knocked on his door. The fact that she knocked got him hard. It meant she was nervous. Did he love her nervous or what?

She opened the door and Sade's breath left him at seeing how she'd dressed. A soft black dress with small straps, letting him see her delicate shoulders. The material hugged her small body all the way down to her feet. He waited for her to turn off the lamp next to his bed and do her thing but instead she sat next to him and gave him a small smile.

What was she up to? Guess he could ask. "What's up?"

"I'm here to help you."

The announcement was innocent, like he really didn't know. He didn't want to rock her boat too badly. "You dressed up," he said.

She gave him a shy smile and looked down at herself. "Not really. Just something comfortable and…"

"Sexy as fuck," he couldn't help.

She regarded him with worried eyes. "It wasn't meant—"

Sure it wasn't. "I didn't think it was," he lied, not wanting to ruin this mood she was trying to create. "You can't help it if you're sexy in everything you wear."

She gave a light snort but the pink in her cheeks said she didn't get those compliments often if ever.

"Okay, well," she glanced toward him then stood. "I'm going to um, kneel between your legs," she said in a soft but instructive tone, "and I'll talk to you while I… help you."

Talk? Jesus this was going to be some kind of trial. Sade's heart thundered as she pulled down the covers and briefly stared at his raging erection before boldly climbing on the bed. Kneeling between his thighs he couldn't help be impressed. Another shiny gold star for his sweet submissive angel.

What would come of her attempts was the question. Maybe him, he really wasn't sure. He hated hand jobs, but with her, everything was different. He couldn't be sure how it would turn out, but so far, he was wagering an orgasm just might be a side effect.

"Okay," she whispered, staring at his chest like she were about to tackle a difficult job. "I'm... not sure how good I am at this."

"I won't judge. But I can't promise you it'll work either."

She looked at him. "Yes, I know." Her tone said she was planning to take the blame if it didn't. She finally got brave enough to look at his cock while lowering her ass to her calves. Very carefully, she placed her hands on his inner thighs and began to stroke there first. She gave a sharp gasp when his cock jumped.

"I think it's jealous," Sade muttered, rather glad for that.

"I want to... work towards it." Her gaze slowly rose up to his chest. "You have a beautiful body," she said.

The unexpected breathless words made his cock jerk hard. "Is that part of your planned speech to help me?"

She looked at him, her hands still stroking his skin. "It was. Yes."

At seeing she worried it was a stupid idea, he said, "Go on then. Keep talking."

She suddenly reminded him of a little girl on her first bike, learning to ride against the wind. Sade wanted more than ever to teach her new tricks.

He felt compelled to help now. "Do you really think that?"

"Yes."

Excitement gripped his cock at her gasped answer, soft stroking fingers, and direct gaze. "Touch it," he whispered, holding her stare tight to his, silently willing her to keep the unusual but electrifying connection. "Touch it everywhere."

Her fingers glided slowly to his shaft finally and Sade rolled his hips for it. She took hold of it like she was handling a bomb that might go off any second. "Yes," he couldn't keep from saying. He fought to keep his eyes open, wanting to feel, but her gaze was like a firm suction on his cock and balls that had him already breathless and moaning from the heat.

She bit her lip, seeming to struggle with the eye contact too. "You're so... soft. And hard. Like a rock covered in silk."

Sade grit his teeth and pulled his restraints while thrusting his cock into her too delicate touch.

"Am I... doing it good?" Her soft question came with firmer strokes of both hands up and down his length, but stopping short of the throbbing head.

"Yes," he gushed. "So fucking good. Tighter."

She gradually tightened and he thrust his hips nice and slow, mimicking deep strokes while he pulled on his restraints.

"Tighter," he whispered.

Again she obeyed and moved her hands over him from base to the ridge of his cock. God the head burned for her touch.

"Everywhere... touch it everywhere."

She stroked along his cock and let her hand glide over the top. Sade hissed, wanting to open his legs more. "Mercy," he whispered, dizzy with desire and surprise at his body's cooperation. "Yes." He wanted her to know she was doing good. "Don't stop. Do it like that, angel."

Her grip tightened even more and she still held his gaze to his amazement. It was like a staring contest and his dominance refused to back down. Her strokes became fluid and her lips parted with her furrowed brows. All of it burned him. But it was her untouched arousal. Yes, that. She wasn't a virgin, but she'd not experienced pleasure. The idea, no, the craving to inflict a brutal ecstasy on her body made him crazy. It made him know without a doubt that he would find a way to do that, and soon.

"Fuck, yes," he groaned, flicking his hips then rolling them slow, showing her a pace. She caught on and mimicked his moves with her hands.

"Like that?" Her breathy words sent a bolt of fire through his dick. "Is this what you like?" Her gaze locked onto his and he suddenly needed more things he normally wasn't aroused with.

"So fucking perfect Mercy. So good, don't stop. God I want your pretty mouth all over it." Sade could hardly believe he'd said those words much less thought them. But he wanted his cock in her mouth. Deep in her mouth, hitting the back of her tight throat.

Her hand cupped his balls and caressed softly while her other worked the length and head of his cock in firm bold strokes. "Do you like this, Sade?" she whispered.

Fuck, the desire in her voice did it. "Mercy, you're so fucking beautiful. Don't stop touching me, fucking don't stop!" He bucked his hips and watched his cock move quickly in her hand.

"Oh my God!" she gasped. "You… yes," she encouraged. "Do it for me. Come for me, Sade. Just for me."

Just for me. Those *possessive* words brought the firestorm roaring through him. It felt like more than a half a year's worth, much more, like a lifetime. Sade bowed off the bed and he didn't stifle his roar, pulling the restraints hard.

"Oh God," she said in quiet fascination after a bit, her strokes slowing. "Do I stop?"

He fought to get his wind and mind back to speak while his body instinctively continued to fight for her touch. *Stop? Never. Never stop*, is what his body said.

Her hands left him slowly, and the disconnect was so powerful that he let out a painful groan from the sensation.

"I did it," she whispered, sounding proud. "I think I did it good?" Sade's breath shuddered out with relief when she laid next to him and put her head on his chest, holding him. "We did it," she whispered, "together." She snuggled her face into him, the small act spearing him with another round of lethal desire. And this desire was hell bent. It would no longer be denied.

"Shower with me baby," he whispered.

She lifted up and he leaned and kissed her forehead. "Please. Trust me. I need you to."

She was silent for a few moments and laid her head down with a sigh. "Okay."

Chapter Thirteen

Sade showered with her, being a saint the entire time. Harmless. Hardly touching her. He waited until after they were dressed while she chained him to the bed to make his move. It was so quick, all she could do was gasp and stare at him with wide *oh shit* eyes. While she had been getting his bandages, he was making a few adjustments to the restraints. Namely, making it so when she put the restraint on him, he could easily restrain at least one of her arms. Now came the tricky part. The rest of her body.

"Don't fight me baby or I'll hurt you, I don't want to hurt you. But you are going to be restrained. This. Very. Night."

She was breathing heavily now, staring at him, calculating.

"I mean it Mercy," he warned, his hands up.

She suddenly launched *at* him, a move he wasn't anticipating, but close grappling was his forte and he had her pinned in seconds. Not wanting to play around, he pressed his forearm into her throat, choking her out. When he felt her losing strength, he pinned her other arm down and restrained it. The second he did, her foot slammed into his head, sending him reeling. But it was done. That would be her last hit.

He shut her ear-piercing screams when it was obvious she was going for waking the dead. Five more minutes and he had her legs restrained as well. Wide open.

He looked at his arm and wiped the blood from it, showing it to her. "You happy now? Made me fucking open my cut!"

She screamed behind her gag.

"What's that? You don't like being tied up?" He sat next to her. "I can honestly feel your pain baby," he said with feigned empathy. "But don't you worry, I have all sorts of dandy plans to teach you about abnormal sexuality. That way you can honestly *know* what the hell you're dealing with when you fucking mess with me. Sounds like a plan?"

She shook her head.

"Good." He stood, looking around for the bandages and began wrapping his arm. "I'm going to cool off so that I can think clearly and not do anything I might regret. I want this long and drawn out for the best effect on your damaged sexual psyche. So you'll have to be patient."

He held up a hand and nodded. "I know you're as eager as I am baby, but we don't want to fuck up a good thing. I need to take my time with this. Explore your every intimate crevice until I know your needs and desires perfectly. Help you connect your emotions to your sexuality? The way you have been so kindly attempting to do to me? Yeah, let's see how we like that shoe on the other foot. Let's see how sweet Mercy does with connecting her body to her sexuality. Because my wager," he said removing his bloodied shirt, "is you've never had an orgasm in your life." He went to his drawer and pulled out a clean black t-shirt. "But you will. You will now."

He worked the shirt over his head, turning to her. "And I honestly can't wait to see what you look like for that." He gave her a slow smile. "Ohhhh, you are going to beg for it."

She shook her head more.

"Oh yes you will." He climbed on the bed until his gaze was right before hers. "Are you looking at me? Are we connecting? Souls meshing here, baby? Mark my words, Miss Mercy. You will beg. For me. For my touch. Until you're burning for it. We clear?" He saw recognition and understanding in her wide gaze and he smiled. "Now you're understanding me." He leaned to kiss her and she jerked her face away. He sniffed long on her skin then licked her cheek. "I don't usually like to taste women, Mercy," he whispered. "But you..." he opened his mouth and sucked on her cheek bone, giving a shuddering moan at the taste. "I think are the exception with my fucked up desires."

Sade went to the basement, his body humming with a dire eagerness.

To bring this poor angel to her *first* orgasm was his immediate order of business. But how, exactly? He walked around his basement, perusing all the possibilities and options. Was like choosing the sweetest candy in the candy store.

He tried to remember ever pleasuring a woman using such non-standard means. All his tools served his fluctuating and at times unpredictable addictions, but all revolved around pain of some kind. He'd use the kiddie settings for her to start.

He finally selected the Y style nipple-clit clamp with the pain adjusters. He selected several teasing toys, varying in pain, and then selected a mask. The black brocade one, with the scroll design. She'd look so fucking sexy in that. Next he grabbed a candy red ball gag and various slim dildos. Very slim. He wanted to start her small and work her up.

His cock twitched while thinking of being in her pussy. His sadism was ready to serve but the problem with that was his own control. He couldn't make any promises with that and he wasn't ready to break her in that way. Sade grabbed his masochistic gear for himself, just as a buffer in case his sadism got out of hand. This would do for now. If he thought of anything else, he'd come back and get it, she wasn't going anywhere.

He returned to his room and kicked the door shut watching her jump. "Hi baby." He dumped his items on the bed and she strained to see. He sat next to her and she made sounds like she wanted to talk and not scream. "You scream and it's going back on."

She nodded.

He removed the gag and she licked her dry lips. "Sade," she whispered.

"Yes?"

"Please don't do this, you don't need to. I'll do this if you untie me."

"Mercy," he began, leaning over to peer into her gaze. "You looking at me? Remember that man you saw when you stared into my eyes? The nice one? The good one?"

She nodded. "Yes, yes, I do. Very much."

"Then where is your faith?" he asked emphatically. "Don't you trust me?"

"I do, I do." Much nodding.

He leaned away. "Then what are you worried about?"

"I just…"

"You're just scared." He stroked the hair along her face. "Perfectly understandable," he said. "Given your lack of experience, being scared is very normal. But you have zero to be afraid of."

She only stared at him, back to reformulating.

"Do you trust me or don't you?" he challenged. Sade nearly held his breath in the silence. There was something about her trusting him that he needed. "Don't lie to me Mercy. Not about this. Do you trust me?"

She finally barely nodded and he let out a breath. "That's my girl," he said. "Would you like to see the toys I brought?" He turned and got the mask and slid it on her then angled his head. "I knew you'd look delicious in it. This mask was made with you in mind, I think." He stroked her lower lip with his thumb and returned to introducing the items to her.

"You're not putting that shit on me!" she exclaimed when he showed her the nipple-clit clamp.

He regarded her black dress, taught with her spread legs. Reaching under it, he stroked his fingers along her panties.

"Sade, stop!" she gasped, sounding worried.

"Mercy." He angled a gaze at her. "You're pussy is wet all the way through your panties." He lifted the edge and slid his finger over the wet hair, getting a reading of her arousal. "Drenched baby."

Sade stood then. "I'm going to get naked for this if you don't mind. I may want to use my cock if it cooperates. And don't panic but I'm going to cut your dress off. You need the gag for that?"

"No, no," she whispered. "No gag."

"Okay angel, no gag," he reassured, getting the scissors and cutting her dress off. "Panties next," he warned, cutting the outer edges and tossing them aside. He stared at the pretty dark triangle of hair. "I honestly don't normally have a desire for this kind of thing but your pussy captivates me. I'll be right back."

"Where are you going?" she called, anxious.

He went to his bathroom and got everything he needed to shave her. He wanted to see her pussy. Every angle and inch of it. He returned and announced, "I'm going to shave you."

"What?" she gasped.

"It's just hair, Mercy. It'll grow back," he assured calmly.

"But why?"

He looked at her. "So I can see your pussy. I can't see the lips the way I want to. Stop looking at me like I'm going to cut your fucking clit off. Trust, remember?"

She merely stared at him.

"Tell me," he said before he sat.

"Tell you what?"

"That you trust me."

"I already said that. But that doesn't mean I want you to shave my privates! Or do anything else with them."

"Did I not agree to let you help me with my sexuality? Did I?"

"Yes, but—"

"And did you see me complaining and not trusting you? Okay, I complained but I didn't fight you. I may not have agreed with your techniques but I did it."

"This is different!" she hissed.

"I don't think so," he said assuredly. "You fucking raped me with emotional orgasms. Repeatedly. I'm just giving you a physical one, why am I the criminal now?"

"Ohhh you're good, aren't you?"

He grinned and wagged his finger at her. "But I'm right. You know I am. And you also know that you have *issues?*" he raised his brows at her. "Right?"

"What does that mean? Exactly?"

He shook his head. "Are you really going to lay there and pretend that you are not suffering from sexual frigidity?"

She stared at him for many seconds. "Frigidity!?" He could tell her eyes were wide behind the mask. "I mean sure I have a few issues, but frigidity is a harsh term, chilly maybe, in areas."

He threw his head back and laughed at that one.

"But still," she said louder, "this isn't the way to address it."

"It's not?" He sat next to her then and waited, staring at her masked face. "Well?"

"Well what?"

"Tell me how to address it. Since you admit you have that problem, I assume being the good and fair doctor that you are, you also had some kind of therapy for yourself in mind? Mmm…" He winked and nodded at seeing it in her gaze. "You did. Share it."

"Of course I had a plan." She looked forward now. "I was going to… slowly… help myself while… helping you."

"Ohhh, nice one," he widened his eyes. "So while you *forced* me to endure your emotional pleasantries—because I was kind of tied up—you were going to be tackling that issue of receiving pleasure by a man. While I was tied up?" he reminded again.

Her mouth had fallen open in something like offense. "You were a *danger* to yourself! You implied you would finish the job! I did that to protect you!"

"Ahhhh yeah," he said, all smiles. "And while you're protecting me, why not conduct your therapy. Two birds with one stone? Or maybe sweet Miss Mercy was protecting herself."

She tightened her lips and looked at the ceiling before clenching her eyes tight. "Fine!" she blasted. "Okay, I may have been… using that opportunity to help you without hitting my own triggers!" She shot a demonic glare at him and growled, "Is that such a goddamn crime, you piece of shit?"

He raised both hands. "Not at all. And I'm simply returning the favor. See, having you tied up while I launch operation Iceberg Meltdown, I am safe from everything that rattles my cage. No more soft touching, soul connecting, mush gushing hymn singing bullshit."

She stared aghast for several seconds. "I didn't... even sing!" was all she could apparently come up with.

"You did," he assured. "It was all a long sick hymn in my head."

"So shaving my privates is going to help me how, you fucking idiot?"

"Well it helps me see what I'm doing," he said with as much fire. "I can't help that I like your pussy baby. Take it as a compliment."

She stared at the ceiling again. "What are you going to do? After?"

"Would you like me to walk you through it as I go? No surprises?"

She made a disgusted noise. "Walk me through your torture? Are you sick? Of course you are, that was a stupid question. No thank you."

"It won't be torture I prom—"

"For me it is!" she growled.

"You want to share?"

"Share what," she spat.

"Why it's torture for you?"

"Oh yes. I'd like to share that it's not your fucking business."

"Talking may help," he suggested, really wanting to know what happened to give her this issue. An overly eager boyfriend? Or maybe those scars had something to do with it. Getting your ass beat could make one skittish in the physical department, he guessed. It was a hard thing for him to rightly judge since all his comparisons were the exception to the norm.

"I'll remember that when you're back in this spot," she said.

"Ohhhh," he smiled. "You really think that's going to happen?"

"Ohhhh," she mocked back. "I *know* it's going to happen."

He had to laugh. "I'm going to proceed with therapy now, if we're done chatting. Ah fuck, what am I thinking? We should probably chat and do therapy at the same time?"

"Suit your fucking self." She went to mumbling something repeatedly with her eyes closed.

He climbed between her legs now, grinning. "What are you saying, Mercy?"

"None of your business."

"Are you praying? It's okay if you are."

"I'm not praying you... prick!"

"Singing? Humming?"

"Chanting! You've got me chanting, are you happy?"

Sade grinned and placed a towel under her ass and wet the soft hair with a wet washcloth, then added a little coconut oil. "Chanting," he muttered. "Whatever helps. I've done this plenty of times, don't worry."

"You have?" she gasped.

"You forget where I work."

Several choked sounds. "People... get tattoos there?"

"Yep."

"Fucking freaks," she whispered before going back to her worried mutterings.

"What are you chanting?" He stroked over her lips, watching her stomach contract with her strained grunts at his touch. "Relax, baby."

"Relax!" she hissed. "I'm going to kick your fucking teeth down your throat when I'm free."

He chuckled at that, believing it one hundred percent. God, she was so much fucking fun. He opened her lips and began to carefully shave one side. "Your whimpers are making me fucking hard. So are you going to tell me?"

"Tell you what?"

"What you're chanting."

"No!"

"Come on. I'll untie you after I'm done," he offered with a small smile while shaving. "Is it hurting?"

"No it fucking *tickles*! Hurry up! No!" she gasped. "Don't hurry!"

She went back to her chanting as he began shaving the other side, gliding his fingers between her lips, letting it graze that magic button.

"Oh Jesus," she strained.

"I know," he said. "That special spot. You're about to find out what it can do if you don't already know." When he finally got all the hair off, he slid his fingers over the opened folds, ensuring they were entirely smooth. And they were. "Wow, just as I thought. You have a gorgeous pussy baby." He traced the shape of it with his fingers while those little whimpers made her stomach heave. "Your clit is nice and ready too." He touched the tip of it.

"That's enough!" she squealed.

Chapter Fourteen

Sade eyed her heaving tits, nearly flat in this position except for a slight mound. And her nipples. His dick throbbed at how tall they stood. Nothing small about those. Except his favorite one that didn't stand quite so tall and straight. It never failed to amaze him how ridiculously hard he got looking at it.

"Okay." He stared at her pussy again and thought about what toy to use first. The idea to continue exploring with his fingers appealed to him. The rare urge was worth indulging at least until it fizzled out.

Kneeling between her legs, he held the base of his cock while touching her wet entrance with a finger.

"What are you doing?" she whispered, panic in her voice while looking away.

"I'm touching you. With my fingers. More… intimate I was thinking?" She let out several strained gasps as he slid his finger up toward her swollen clit. "Is it hot right here?" He stroked it softly, her squeal making his cock throb. She sank her hips into the bed, trying to evade his touch, only there was nowhere for her to go. He decided to make it even more personal and knelt on the floor next to the bed. "So we can talk during your session," he explained when she dared a look at him. "Soul mesh?"

She jerked away. "I can't! It's too fast," she whispered.

"Slower? Have you ever touched yourself there?"

"No!" Like it was crazy to even think.

"Would you like to bring your first orgasm or would you like me to?"

"Me?"

"Yes, you. It's called masturbating, baby, come on. Surely you know what that is."

"I do! I just... don't do that."

"Make your choice. Me or you."

"Oh God," she whispered, like she were choosing which limb to cut first. "Me."

"You realize I'm not untying you for that?"

"How would I do it then?" she said annoyed.

"I'd tie the chain on your preferred hand to the foot board."

She gave a few frustrated grunts.

"Well?"

"You do it," she barely said.

His dick pulsed with her answer. "Good choice. And just so you know this isn't easy for me."

"Oh please."

"I'm in a lot of pain enduring this for you."

"Which turns out perfect for you, doesn't it!"

"Yes, thankfully," he chuckled. "One time occasion when my sickness rescues me." Sade stroked her puckered folds again, a slow spreading of her juices everywhere but on her clit. "I'll let you not look at me for now," he said, circling the hard bud, leaning until his nose hit her cheek. "Mmmm." He let his finger tease on her clit, a slow swirl right over the edge. "Feel that? Let it get hot right here."

Her chest heaved with sporadic straining and moans escaping. He stared at her breasts now. "Your tits are so tight baby." He let his finger slide lower to her opening. "Can I touch your nipples, Mercy?"

She strained and grunted but didn't answer.

He went back to stroking her clit, turning up the fire with slow flicks of his finger until her body shuddered and made all those delicious sounds of resistance. "Don't fight it baby, let the heat come." He stroked his finger over the nearest nipple—his favorite one. She let out a gasp as her body began to betray her more. "I just want to show you how good it can feel, I'm not going to hurt you. Which I'm surprised about since you toyed with my sadism. Did you know I was thinking of fucking you because of that?"

She didn't answer as Sade rolled her nipple between his fingers.

"I know I said I can't get my dick hard in a woman's pussy and I didn't lie," he said, delivering rapid flicks on her clit until she gasped. "But I don't like to fuck them. Not like that. It's not really nice what I do, and I think I'm actually a nice guy. "He wiggled two fingers rapidly over her clit, making her moans peak before backing off. "But you..." He slid his middle finger to her opening and played just in the entrance. "I actually want to shove my cock in you. But… it seems I especially don't want to hurt you." He twirled the tip at her opening, slow and teasing. "Can I put my finger in you, angel?"

She let out several gasps and strained moans before that one word finally wrenched out of her. "Yes!"

His own breath shuddered out as he pressed his cock into the side of the bed and slid just inside her slowly, closing his eyes. "I knew you'd be hot and tight. I'm going very fucking slow for you." His mind made the perfect transference to his dick and it throbbed hard. Her hips slowly moved for it now. "You're fucking my finger angel, that's good. I fucking wish so much that you could handle my sadism." He held the top of her head, gripping a handful of silky hair while lowering his mouth to her breast. "Nobody can handle it," he muttered as he moved his lips over her hard nipple and slowly penetrated her pussy.

"Mercy," he whispered at the profound noises she made. He had to ask her at least, just to hear. "Would you take my cock when it's angry?" His middle finger was all the way in and he placed his thumb on her clit next. She was finally past that inhibition and he didn't need to move it—she did all the work, pumping against his hand.

"Sade," she gasped. "Sade yes!"

He allowed the answer to mean yes, she would like it. He opened his mouth wide and sucked as much of her pretty tit as he could, flicking his tongue quickly over the tip of that nipple while she bucked and thrashed on his hand. Sade growled, moving his finger deep inside her, his sadism a wild fire. She suddenly turned her face toward him and he hurried to those lips, licking them as she screamed her first fucking orgasm. But it was his name that she constantly gasped with every breath and the way she fought to kiss him that did it for him. Did it so fucking strangely and perfectly.

"Fuck, Mercy," he whispered when it was over and she was back to looking away from him. "You did so very good, so fucking good."

Her only answer was breathless tiny whimpers. Sade was delirious with that strange desire and all its strange compelling. He hurried to obey the need to lay between her legs, curious as to how far she could take him. He'd crossed over into another sexual dimension and was open to whatever awaited, eager to go with it as long as his body allowed.

He smelled her orgasm and waited to see what it would do to him. The urge to smell more thoroughly brought his nose sliding along her wet lips. Then it wasn't enough to smell her. "I need to taste you Mercy," he whispered, astonished. "Can I taste you?" It was an act of pure nobility on his part to ask. Not something he needed to do or wanted, but did for her sake.

She answered with those whimpers, making him impatient. He took his first lick, just a tiny one while waiting. But when her essence hit his tongue, more of that new hunger slammed him to have it all, in that second. "Mercy," he whispered, dizzy with it. He licked from the bottom of her pussy up to her clit, capturing all of her essence onto his tongue.

She let out a shocked moan that struck his sadism. She'd not been licked that way before. His tongue was her first. He began to eat her pussy with a reckless hunger, something he'd never done to a woman before, never wanted to. "Fuck yes!" he gasped, spreading her lips open more with his fingers to get at the inner silk. He dipped inside her and the succulent heat gripped his tongue with her cry. Sade forgot all about pace and buried his tongue deeper, pressing his nose into her wet clit. Jesus *Christ* she fucking tasted *and* smelled insanely good.

Sade felt a new addiction quickly setting in as he slid his lips all over hers and sucked them into his mouth. He was astonished. He didn't even like to kiss, but kissing her pussy was suddenly the kink of fucking kinks. He growled and angled his head, his lips and tongue, even teeth in on the feast. He moved so he could finger her, God he wanted to feel her pussy clamping on him in any way while he sucked her.

"Sade, oh God, yes."

"Mercy, Mercy," he moaned on her bucking pussy while working his finger in her again.

She cried out and flicked her hips on his mouth. "Yes, yes," she gasped. "Please yes."

He buried his lips in her folds and sucked her clit into his mouth.

"I need you, I need you," she gasped. "Do it."

He didn't let go of her clit as he answered with a deep groan, moving his finger in and out of her faster, then rained fire on her clit with flicks of his tongue.

She cried out long and sweet. "Sade, don't... don't stop."

Oh he wasn't. He fucking wasn't.

Her cries peaked again and Sade reached up and pinched her nipple while he sucked harder on her clit.

Her orgasm erupted instantly in waves of loud shrill moans that detonated a heat bomb in his cock until he thought it would burst. He finally crawled his way over her body and straddled her chest. "You're going to suck my cock."

He wasn't shocked to hear her gasp, "Yes!" and lean for it. Giving was easier than receiving for her and her eagerness burned him.

He held her head forward and rubbed the head on her lips, watching her open hungrily for it. "Suck me Mercy," he whispered. "You've been wanting this baby?"

"Yes, yes!" She licked him all over making his groan explode out.

"Your mouth looks so good on my cock baby, I knew it fucking would. I don't let women suck me Mercy. I need to go deep. I need your teeth all over it, I need it against your throat."

She opened for it, leaning for more. Sade braced his hands on the wall before him and began moving slowly in and out of her mouth, hissing with the painful scrape of her teeth. She looked up the line of his body and watched him. Sade was sucked into her gaze as he began moving faster. When he felt his orgasm, he didn't stop it like he normally would when his sadism was engaged. He didn't want to traumatize her right off, but the fantasy of having her for his sadistic fuck was quickly reaching the top of his needs list. "I'm coming baby, take it, take it all."

Her nose fluttered as he bucked his hips but the heat and desire for him in her eyes brought his raging orgasm. He felt her fucking *swallowing* him as he pumped long and slow now, his harsh groans mingling with her delicate ones all over his cock.

He carefully removed himself and collapsed onto the bed, eyes closed for the longest time, gasping in the aftermath of what had just happened, what had never happened before. He finally looked at her and at seeing an odd look in her eyes—longing he'd like to think, he turned on his side and propped his head on his hand, staring down at her. "Are you mad at me?"

She turned her head away.

Fuck. The urge to make it up to her brought his lips to her ear. "Please don't be mad at me, Mercy."

"Untie me then."

He moaned. "Not yet."

"Why not?"

"Because one session isn't enough. You'll need quite a few."

She jerked her gaze to him. "Well I need to pee!"

He leaned in and stole a quick kiss before she could head butt him for it. She was pissed enough to. Maybe.

"What else is there?"

He didn't miss the tiny bit of curiosity in her tone, even though he was sure she didn't know it was there. "Ohhh Mercy," he whispered. "So much more I think. I need to do things to you. In different positions. Until you're well versed in sexual play."

"I'm not supposed to sexually play with a man I'm not in love with. See that's what you need to learn."

In love? Wow, of all her delusions, that had to be the most fucking precious. He couldn't resist a smile either at how she always made it about emotions. "I need to learn that?"

"Yes, you do," she muttered.

"Are you going to teach me that too, Mercy?" He leaned in and rubbed his lips along her cheek.

"You'd have to want to learn, for one."

"I do, I do want to learn," he said in all honesty. But he was sure it wasn't even possible to teach if it did actually exist. "Can you teach that? Wouldn't you need to know love too?"

She turned halfway to him. "Um. I *do* know that," she said with light sarcasm.

"You do?" He found even her anger adorable. "You're such a bad liar." He thought about that. "I like seeing you do bad things. Would you consider letting me use you in my sadistic fucking?"

She jerked to him fully with angry green eyes. "Are you referring to your sexathons?"

He raised his brows. "I call them sexorcisms. Who told you? Bo? That little shit has a big mouth."

"Yes, but don't blame him! It slipped when you tried to kill yourself, he was shaken. And no I don't want to be a *fuck* for your anything!"

He traced his finger on her shoulder, amazed that she had the ability to think of Bo's well-being at that moment. "I didn't think you would. Tabitha usually helps arrange those."

"What? Why?"

"Don't worry, it's not just Tabitha in those. I have to use more than one woman."

"Oh. My. God," she whispered. "That is just so wrong, Sade."

"I don't like it either."

"Then why do it?"

"I rarely do." He laid on his back, amazed that he wasn't more upset while talking about the despised thing.

"Then just quit!"

"I keep it back as long as I can but sometimes I have to. It's been a while, I know my body. Soon, I'll need to do it." He turned his head and studied her shocked face. "I'm not proud of them if that helps. It's not my thing to use women in any way they don't want. I pay them well and that's the little excuse I use to make fucking them senseless all okay."

"Sade listen to me. There are ways to deal with this. Can you take this stupid mask off?"

He looked at her, liking her in the mask. "Deal with needing to fuck while I'm angry?"

She made incredulous noises. "Yes! I mean… you can make love to one woman and she can help you with that."

He turned on his side again, getting close enough to feel the breath of her strange words, knowing they'd be a turn on in some new way. "She could help with that?"

"Why are you smiling like that?"

"Because I find you so fucking adorable with your emotional words and terms for everything."

"Emotions are a real part of people and even if you hide yours, you still have them."

"I know they are. And I do have them, just not all of them when fucking. I do have a lot of anger though. I know that."

"But you *should* have all of them… well… not anger so much, when you're fucking."

He smiled. "You said fucking."

"I'm serious, Sade."

"So making love," he continued, "do you have to be in love for this?"

"Well yes," she cried.

"I'm messing with you, angel. Is it bad to you that I don't know how to be that?"

"No, no, it's not bad," she nearly cooed. This time the mush touched him since she said it while tied up being molested by him. Her fucking kindness was… baffling. "I think you maybe do know and you don't realize you do."

He kissed on her shoulder, wanting to feel her skin on his lips again. "You get major points for making me even consider it. But really, I'm not interested in love."

"Then you're not interested in me," she exclaimed.

"Wrong," he said. "I am so… very fucking interested in you." He traced the mound of her breast and her breath sucked in. "And I think you must love me. You respond so nicely to my touch."

"I can't help that, you're forcing it."

"Ohhh no, no. I know very well the difference between embraced pleasure and forced. And even though you have a hard time with it at first… you embrace it like a vice on my cock."

She turned her face away.

He leaned and covered her nipple with his mouth, getting lost in the feel of the thick tip along his teeth, rolling his tongue and lips over it. He flicked over the very top and moaned at the way she arched her back and strained not to tell what it did. "See baby? You love my touch. Why do you fight it?"

"Because it's forced!" she whined a little, while straining.

"Force doesn't have to be bad." He stroked along her inner thigh, listening to her quickened breaths. He barely touched her open folds, learning the delicious true story. "You're dripping again."

She strained in silly denial. "From before," she barely whispered.

He spread her juices very slowly around her clit. "Pretty sure I licked all that up." He danced his touch near his target. "Mercy. Look at me. Talk to me."

She gave a small shake of her head with a tiny peep sound.

"You were so right about chitchatting and intimacy. I like this fucking connection." He said this while stroking softly on her clit. "Come on angel," he urged, "look at me while I touch you here. The sooner you learn it, the faster you pass."

She jerked her face to him and seeing the heat mingling in her angry gaze made him shudder in anticipation.

"This right here?" He rubbed slow circles over it. "Don't stop looking at me." He leaned to her mouth, feeling her gasps. He licked along the top of her lip. She cried out, a sound of perfect torment as he built her fire. "Maybe you actually can play with me. Somebody you don't love."

He plunged his finger deep inside her before she could argue, taking her sharp cry of his name right in his mouth, letting it tear a fiery path through his rules, desires, addictions. For the first time in his life that he could remember, pleasure without pain came together for a dance. He plunged his tongue now, his growls hungry, hungry to bring his fury to the stage and blow her away. "Dance for me angel," he rasped.

"Sade! Yes, God yes!," she said in fucking beautiful abandon. "Touch me, touch me, kiss me," she cried frantic.

The desperate need in her voice… with his name connected… Fucking confounding. And if she'd said *fuck me* he'd have his cock inside her so very deep. But he had to hear that one before he crossed that barrier of no return. Once he did that, he would lose himself to that anger and fuck her to pieces. With a gasp, he pulled his finger out and made war on her hard clit.

"Come for me, Mercy," he said in her mouth as he gave her sweet clit three hard spanks. Her reaction made him crazy, sharp cries of *yes*. "You like that, fuck," he whispered, thrusting his finger deep, his need for that angry reckless in the rapid jabs. "Of course you do," he shuddered. "Such a beautiful angel." He pulled out and wiggled his touch over her clit until her body bowed up with the pleasure. He fucked her mouth with his tongue then lifted up, looking at her. "I'm going to spank your clit till you come. Would you like that?"

She locked her gaze on his. "Yes, yes!"

He slapped it twice and she jolted with it. "You like that?" He popped it a few more times. "Tell me!" he rasped, ready to tear into her in some manner.

"Yes!"

"Beg for it, beg me," he ordered, spanking more.

"Please make me feel good!"

He spanked non-stop, softly at first then increased speed and pressure until her screams peaked and her body broke in violent shudders. He growled and pressed his palm on her clit, letting her buck against the constant pressure while he tasted the ecstasy in every breath, every plea and beg, biting at her lips.

Her orgasm spiraled down and she panted with her eyes closed, facing him still. Sade gasped from the rush and kissed along her face, not getting why he did, why he'd even want to do the oddity or why the urge was becoming frequent with her. He only knew that everything about her demanded it, and it seemed perfectly right to obey before it disappeared like so many other near pleasures that didn't require some form of fucking pain.

He laid on his back now, longing to untie her. Feel her on him, touching him back. What would that be like? Both of them touching at the same time during such an unusual connection? Part of him was leery to find out, which compelled him all the more.

"I need the bathroom," she said in a tiny voice.

Right. Fuck. She could go like she made him go. Tied to a chain.

"Can't you untie me now? I'm pretty sure I'm used to it."

Yeah right. He'd need to be sure and he was far from it.

"You can tie me back up if I'm wrong."

"Because you'd so let me."

"I would."

"And I know that how?"

"I give you my word!"

He couldn't help but laugh. And laugh. And laugh.

"It's not even that funny!"

And laugh.

"Sade! I need to *pee!*"

"You can use the same chain as you made me."

"I am *not* the same threat as you!"

"I wasn't a threat."

"To yourself! You nearly died!"

"Yeah and you *stopped it*. Like you stopped Tabitha, like you stopped me from fighting. Block, block, block Sade's need for pain. Thank you Miss *Mercy!*"

"Well you're *very* welcome Mr. *Sade*! And I'll do it again and again and again! And again!"

"I bet you would." He sat up, not sure why that didn't really piss him off any more. "So if I untie you… you'll still do sexual therapy with me?"

She didn't answer and Sade looked back at her to find her staring. Thinking.

"That you have to think so long says no."

"I just don't want to agree to something I can't follow through with!"

"Then we should do a few more rounds."

"No! No, no! Fine I'll do it. If you…"

"Let you lead?"

"Yes! Yes, that. I can handle that."

"If you don't, I'm going to wrestle you back into these restraints."

"You won't need to, I'll go willingly."

Hmph. He kinda hoped she defied him. He liked hard physical contact with her too. "Hold still then."

Chapter Fifteen

"Ohhhh thank you, thank you," she whispered as he began untying her. "You won't regret this."

When she was finally free, he eyed her, ready. She removed the mask to his disappointment and pulled the covers over her. She glanced toward him. "What? I can still be shy can't I?"

Fuck, just what did he love so much about that? "Yes, please do."

She looked down and to the right then back toward him. "You like me shy?"

At seeing she was that interested in what he liked about her, at that moment, brought his grin. "I think I do. Very much so."

"I'm going to the bathroom now."

"I'm following you."

"Fine."

Her light tone made him cautious. He hoped it was genuine because if it was, then that meant she'd accepted him. And the idea that she would, did those strange things to him that accompanied all her little magic tricks.

He leaned in the doorway, watching her sit on the toilet. "Please!" she exclaimed.

He rolled his eyes and pushed off the doorjamb, waiting in the hall. He didn't entirely trust her.

She appeared in the doorway a few moments later and stared at him. "Can I get dressed?"

He stepped aside and she went to her room while he went to the kitchen. Fuck he was hungry. When she came out, he was biting into an apple. He eyed her clothes. "You uh, gonna be working out?"

"Yep."

By the time she roundhouse kicked the apple out of his hand, he'd lost the precious seconds that would give him some kind of advantage. She barraged him with kicks and punches until Sade found himself in the corner of the kitchen, leg up and shielding his side, arms over his face. "Mercy! Stop it!"

"Come on!" she screamed at him. "Fight me! You want to tie me up? I'll show you motherfucker, you're getting it!"

Sade launched for her and they hit the floor. Unlike the last time they grappled, she got the upper hand first. He realized exactly how serious she was when her fist made quite a few solid connections to his face, triggering his anger.

He roared and flipped her off, feeling warm leaking onto this lip. He wiped with his arm. "Fucking busted my nose?"

"That's not all I'm going to bust baby!"

Shit. She meant it. The idea that he'd have to hurt her was more than he could stand. She ran at him with a yell and he did the only thing he could think in that second. He ran to his basement.

She was hot on his heels and busted through the door before he could lock her out. "Mercy, stop!"

"I am *so* going to love kicking your *motherfucking ass*!" She ran at him and he dodged only to get a quick back fist in the head.

Sade grabbed a flogging staff and held it at her. "Don't make me hurt you baby."

"You can't hurt me more than you have!" she screamed, running at him.

Sade again evaded, eyeing the door.

"I'll bite your ear off before you can open it," she seethed.

"Mercy," he held his free hand up. "Truce, come on. I'll let you tie me up if you want to. Just… calm down."

"I won't calm down!" she screamed, looking right and grabbing something and throwing it at him. "I won't calm down you bastard! You made me!" She snatched up whatever she could get her hands on and launched it at him, making him dodge the onslaught.

Fuck, she was beyond furious. "I'm sorry, I am!"

"I'm sorry!" she continued screaming. "I'm sorry, I'm the sorry one! Me! The stupid girl!" She grabbed wildly for things, not even seeing. "Stupid little girl! Stupid scars!" She ran at him and he grabbed her in his arms. The fight he expected didn't come as she suddenly hung limp in his embrace with light wailing. "Stupid scars," she gasped.

"I'm sorry Mercy," he whispered, panicked at feeling the depth of her pain. It was so fucking deep and had less to do with what he'd done. It was about something else. Those scars. Those fucking scars. What the fuck? God, what happened to her? "I'm sorry baby," he gasped in her ear. I mean it, I'm so sorry."

"They cut me," she wailed the words with a long sob before gasping, "They made me cry all the time, every day. Over and over and over they… they *put* things in me," she barely whispered. "I can't have a family, I can't ever be a mother!"

Fury trembled through Sade at her words. She'd been raped? Repeatedly? The idea that she'd lived a hell like him made him grip her tight in dread. That he'd done what he had to her made him sick now. A little girl, an angel, hurt and confused by the same evil that had hurt him and he'd done that? "I was only four," she gasped. "Then five and six! Seven, eight, nine and ten!"

"Oh fuck," he gasped, clenching his eyes tight. "Oh God," he growled bitterly, "I'm so sorry." He stroked her head.

"Nobody to hate," she cried hoarsely, limp in his arms. "The faces changed, they always changed. They changed, they recycled me…" she barely wailed, "they recycled me, Sade. Recycled my life away, and all my stupid little girl dreams."

Sade let out a roar of fury as he gripped her hard. "I'm so fucking sorry," he said, the pain suffocating him. "I didn't know."

"I know," she wailed. "I know you didn't know. But I'm broken," she cried into his shoulder. "My body is so broken and it won't *fix*. I thought I fixed it but I didn't," she cried confused and lost. "I just want you to touch me so bad and I can't," she gripped him back tight now. "I want to help you and I can't. I can't, my body is dirty and broken!"

"I got you," he whispered, hugging her tight while rocking her side to side a little. "I got you, I'll help you baby. You're not dirty, you're so fucking beautiful. I'll fix it, you'll see."

****

Sade lay awake numb all night, replaying the words she'd screamed at him, wishing he could shut them off. He could only wonder what exactly her confession would do to him. Something. They were doing something big and bad, he could feel it. He wasn't sure what and he didn't like not knowing. He just knew that Mercy was… *his*. His in a way he didn't really get, only knew she was. And he wanted her. He had to have her. Every bit of her. Own her. Whatever the fuck that even meant or looked like, that's what was happening. Maybe it was her misery and pain that he had to have. He loved all forms of it and having sweet little Mercy's pain and suffering to take into himself was nothing short of utopia for his fucked up kinks. He got his sadomasochistic cake and he got to devour it too.

****

Mercy smiled, unsure why she should be happy since she'd officially lost her marbles on Sade yesterday. She just felt… free and… safe. Yeah. Safe. The way he'd hugged her so tight. She felt her pain enter him, it was an odd knowing, or sensation to feel him absorbing it, sharing it with her. Sharing. That's what it was that had her smiling. The only other man who'd made that hard exchange with her pain had been her father.

She'd shared that darkness with him and the freedom it came with was a little shocking. He knew she was broken now. And he was okay with it. Loved her anyway? Love might be a strong word but… she felt it. With him. Even if he didn't know it.

She remembered the things he'd *made* her do. She bit her lip as she pranced around the house like Cinderella with her happy duster. She wasn't at all unhappy about what he'd done with her really. She'd planned to work her way to that and while it wasn't her preferred method, she understood him and his. And okay, yes, she'd definitely fantasized about it. Not in that way but of him touching her, doing things. He was very gentle. Perfect.

She'd really only intended to let him know how she felt about the whole forced thing and lost her temper when her past jumped in. Then came the pain, and helpless rage. It was a cycle she used to go through and it snuck up on her. But she knew Sade wouldn't have done any of it had he known her secret. And even now, she worried he might not ever touch her again with the way he treated her. Like she were breakable. And he was the devil.

She'd have to convince him that she was okay. And that he wasn't the monster. She had ideas to do that. Heat filled her privates and made them tingle just like they had while she'd touched him and when he'd... done those amazing things to her. She liked it so much. Liked touching him even more. Liked him touching her less, right at first, but once it felt so good… then God yes.

She smiled, never dreaming she'd ever be able to touch a man in that way without being sucked into past nightmares. He was just… so different than anybody and anything she'd been around in that respect. Those monsters never cared about her. And while Sade wasn't exactly what she'd call a gentleman, there was this fierceness in him that wouldn't allow her to be hurt. She believed that, felt it. Knew she was safe with him.

So what to do now? She was ready to continue on with their dual therapies. Helping him and herself at the same time. Her leading. Him letting.

Would be nice if she knew she were doing things right. Maybe she could ask him. Would be a good way to make those intimate connections. He was very good at looking into her eyes. Better than her even. Probably a challenge for him that he couldn't resist.

She turned from the wall of glass in the living room and gasped at finding Sade leaning against the wall, arms crossed over his naked chest. Watching her. "Hi," she flopped a wave. "I uh..." she tossed a thumb toward the kitchen, "cooked. Guess what I made?"

He took his time answering. "What?" he asked softly, staring intently at her until butterflies went crazy in her stomach.

"Lasagna."

He waited a moment before saying, "I fucking *love*... lasagna."

She bit a smile at the way it felt, like he meant her. That he loved her. She lowered her head smiling. "Good. I'm so very glad you *love* it."

"Are you." He pushed off the wall and approached with a stride and look that set her heart racing.

She could only nod when he finally stopped just before her, angling his head. "The bed is cold. Mercy." She swallowed down the butterflies that his deep, sexy voice caused and resisted the urge to clam up. He stroked her face with a finger, so very softly and then paused. "I'm scaring you."

Mercy latched on to his hand before he could lower it. "No. Not really." She pressed it to her face, suddenly wanting to cry at the idea that he would feel rejected and not touch her anymore. "Please," she whispered. "Help me."

He stared into her eyes again, looking tormented. "I…"

She waited and encouraged, "What? Tell me."

"Want to kiss you."

"Okay," she whispered, biting her lower lip at the explosion of butterflies again.

"I don't usually… want to kiss," he said, seeming confused.

Again she nodded, pain stabbing her. "Okay. You don't have to."

"No, I mean… I don't understand why I want to. When I never liked it before."

She smiled, back to hopeful. "Because it's me," she whispered.

"You?" he narrowed his gaze as it roamed her face. "And who are you?"

Her smile faded as his mouth slowly lowered. "Mercy," she whispered, closing her eyes as his lips slid so softly over hers.

"Mercy," he murmured, one hand stroking her jaw and the other sliding behind her neck.

She placed her hands on his warm chest and his hot breath flooded her mouth as his lips pressed softly into hers. She gasped and without thought, her hands began to explore his silky muscles. They ventured over his sides and circled his waist then roamed up his thick back. He was so hard and hot to the touch.

Sade's breath shuddered and he kissed deeper, his tongue stroking carefully and sweetly along hers, his hands roaming her backside with an urgency. She locked her arms around his neck, straining to get more of him in her mouth, tasting with an equal hunger, moaning her need for more. His hand buried between her ass and squeezed hard, pulling her up his body.

Their moans of hunger mingled, rough and delicate as she wrapped her legs around his waist. "I want to suck you… in the shower."

His breath rushed out and he growled walking blindly with her in that direction. Once in the bathroom, he quickly undressed and Mercy was suddenly awestruck with his nudity. A mix of desire and fear throbbed between her legs and tightened the bottom of her stomach. He went into the shower and turned it on, giving her full view of his delicious backside.

She quickly undressed before she lost her nerve, assuming he'd turned to give her that opportunity of privacy. She hurried in and stepped discreetly to the right and waited in the corner of the steamy square, forearms over her misshaped breasts.

He began washing his hair and then body, with an ease like she weren't there gawking and watching his every move, studying his every shiny curve and… large… thick… penis. Her mouth suddenly watered while the tingle in her privates quickened her breaths. She remembered what he felt like all the way in her mouth, how he looked moving in and out, how his stomach muscles—all his muscles stood out with the effect she had on him. She did that.

She realized he was staring at her and she jerked her gaze up from her fantasy. "Did you like it yesterday?" he asked.

She nodded, holding her arms tighter to her chest, her eyes riveted to his.

"Talk to me. What do you want?"

"You," she whispered, not afraid of that.

His eyes rolled shut and his brows furrowed as he lowered his head. Mercy noticed at that moment that his penis… wasn't so huge. What was wrong? Did she say the wrong thing?

"Suck you," she said, hoping to fix it.

He didn't answer at first, he just stared silently at her. "What else," he said. "Tell me."

His deep voice lured things in her she wasn't familiar with, but she was also afraid he was wanting something specific and she would get it wrong. Past memories that involved guess work and ended in brutal sexual punishment clawed at her mind. "I..." she blinked and cleared her throat, watching his face become a mask of confusion. "You wanted me to..."

"Say it," he gasped.

His desperation stole the words from her mind and she felt her mouth trying to work, hoping it would just say it for her, remember for her. "You uh..." She closed her eyes. "I..."

His arms were suddenly around her with *shhhhhh*ing in her ear. She trembled with a violence. "You're okay baby. I'm here. I'm sorry, fuck. You don't have to answer." He stroked her head against his chest, an adoring and protective stroke that made her fears untangle from her stomach. She wrapped her arms around him, still shaking.

He turned with her into the hot water and they stood that way in silence for a long time. Then he tilted her head back and wet her hair, his gaze hungry on her face as he lathered shampoo in it. His fingers massaged her scalp with sensual strokes that brought a calm over her. She closed her eyes and let herself enjoy it, his soapy hands gliding down her neck and over her shoulders and arms. Then her hands were carefully cleansed, each of her fingers with his. He turned her into the shower and placed her back against him, his touch gliding over stomach and very carefully over her breasts, making her breath hitch. His other hand slid over her privates, barely touching the folds before stroking with a firm hunger over her inner thighs. Mercy lifted a leg, wanting him to know she needed it.

His mouth pressed onto her ear with harsh breaths as his finger teased over her ugly nipple. She hated that he seemed to favor it and tried not to think about how it got that way. He made it easy, sliding his finger between her folds to toy with her clit. She whimpered and reached up, latching her arms around his neck. He abandoned her nipple and sat on the seat in the corner. Holding her hand, he pulled her onto his lap so that she faced him, draping her legs on either side. He looked between them and in continued silence, stroked his finger up and down her wet opening. He looked into her face. "Look at me," he said to her.

She met his gaze, feeling dizzy, holding onto his shoulders. With a slow gentleness, he worked his finger all the way deep inside. She fought not to roll her eyes shut and just feel but she let the moans come, telling him how good it felt.

"Touch yourself for me."

His words rumbled with hot harshness. She knew where to touch by now. He'd certainly made that spot well known. She even knew how to touch it. She mimicked his circular motions over the spot that was aching and hot, still maintaining eye contact while giving moaned gasps.

"Feels good baby?"

The desire in his velvety tone and the slow in and out strokes of his finger was more than she could stand with her eyes open.

"That's good baby, feel it. Feel it perfectly. Your pussy is so wet and the fucking smell is delicious. Did you know I like the taste of you? I do. God, I do. I've never liked the taste of any woman, did you know that?"

She rubbed faster circles, crying out more. "Yes, taste me," she whispered. "So hot."

"It's hot baby?"

"Sade, yes." Her mouth refused to shut now, it remained open with constant moans. "Faster Sade. Do it faster."

"Fuck, Mercy."

The angle of his voice said he was looking down as he moved in and out faster.

"Do it, yes, do it." Her own assault over that hard bud filled her with a heat until she had that pee feeling. She gave a sharp gasp when it broke through, then shrieked.

"Come my sweet angel," he growled, his finger working in and out so very fast now. She gripped his neck with one hand and bucked in his lap. "Listen to how wet you are, fuck," he gasped.

She suddenly kissed him, thrusting her tongue in his mouth with frantic moans until the final electrical pulses subsided and all that was left was her repeated *oh God oh God's.*

He suddenly pulled her into his embrace and held her so tight to his body that she could feel the pounding of his chest.

"Your turn," she whispered.

Chapter Sixteen

His turn. Right. Sade gripped her head tight with one hand. "Fuck baby."

She fought to pull back. "What? What's wrong?"

He put his forehead on hers and shook it. "I don't know."

"Talk to me," she said, worried.

"It's gone." The words rushed out in a whisper.

She scanned his body. "What? What's gone? Are you hurt?"

"No, I'm not hurt, I'm just… I can't…" He shook his head and she climbed off his lap. He stood and turned, confused. "It's gone. I can't fucking explain it. I think about you now and all my desire leaves my dick."

She gasped. "What?"

He turned to her. "No, it's not what that sounded like. I mean… I think about you and," he put his hand on his chest and slid it around. "The heat is all here. I'm fucked up, I knew this. We both knew this, nothing works right on me." He held his head now. "But how can I go from you making me so fucking hard I can come by looking at you, to not being able to get hard at all? Why!"

She stared at him, her doctor look on. "When did this start?"

"I don't fucking know." He paced in the steam now.

"Since... I told you about what happened?"

He scrubbed his hands over his face, eyeing her. "Maybe." But that was definitely when. Everything started to change at that point.

"Maybe," she gasped. "My past disgusts you! I disgust you!"

"No, no, no," he wagged a finger. "Not true, not remotely true." She stared hard at him and he continued to shake his head. "Not that."

"Then what?"

He shrugged hard and long. "Good fucking question."

She yelped when he spun and hit the shower wall with his fist then shook it. "Don't do that!" she cried.

"Why can't my life give me a break, why can't my body give me a fucking break! I finally find something I like and want so bad but *fuck no!* Fuck no Sade, you can't *have it!* Something *good* and fucking *beautiful!*" His voice went hoarse and he covered his face with both hands. "Fucking beautiful, you know?" He looked down, shaking his head. "Everything about you Mercy... is beautiful," he croaked. "And I want it so bad, Mercy. I fucking want you... every last bit of you... so bad."

"Okay," she whispered around a sob. "You've got me," she reassured, going into his arms and hugging him. "We'll figure this out, you and me, ok? Just like anything. We'll fix it."

Sade held tight to her. Held tight to the thing he wanted and his body refused to let him have. Fucking past. No matter how well he bowed to its evil wicked scars it never gave an inch back. One good decent feeling was too much. One decent *normal* desire was too fucking much.

Sade's jaw tightened in fury and he welcomed the familiar power. He wasn't going to lay down and accept that he couldn't have what he wanted. He wanted Mercy. He wanted her even if it meant having her in his prison of pain and fury. Just so he had every bit of her.

****

"I got it!" Mercy's sudden words jerked Sade out of sleep. She sat up and shook him.

"I'm up, what?" He reached out for her, not liking the absence of her warm body.

"I figured it out!"

Always the therapist, even in sleep. "What out? Damn what time is it?"

"Not sure. But you know how my body freezes up in fear?"

Sade reached for the light on the lamp and switched it on.

"And how yours likes pain with pleasure?" she asked.

"Uhhh yeah?"

"Duh!" she exclaimed with a gasp of excitement and a smack on his shoulder. "Our bodies are *tricked!*" she squealed in triumph. "Mine shuts down in fear when sexually stimulated, yours shuts down when *emotionally* stimulated!"

He regarded her now up on his elbows. "How… is this exciting news?"

She gave a choked snort. "Well knowing is half the battle, I think? It puts us at least with what the problem is."

"Maybe."

"I'd bet on it, it makes perfect sense. Your body doesn't know anything but pain with pleasure."

"And anger," he added, collapsing onto his back and closed his eyes. "You weren't exactly causing me pain when I was having that pleasure."

"But what happened in here Sade when I told you my story?" She touched his chest.

He looked at her and held her hand to him. "Shattered. I think."

"Aww, that's sweet. But no! It *connected* with *me!*" She kicked her legs with happy squeals and dove on him. "You *like me so much you can't get aroused!*" She kissed him, square on the lips, still wiggling all over on him. "Oh my God that's so awesome!"

Sade's hands roamed over her, waiting for his body to get off to some part of this, any part of it. But the only response was his need to blow her mind with pleasure. "How is that awesome?" He gripped her exactly between her ass, pressing his finger on plump softness. Her sharp intake of breath gave his dick a shot of desire.

"Well maybe not to you but to me! I wanted you to like me like that," she whined with the sweetest tone. And just like that, the heat left his dick and went to his chest. Clearly the two were in a war for her. Neither willing to share, leaving Sade the helpless bystander to his body's mysterious sick ways.

He pulled her tight onto his body. "It's doing it now."

"It is?" she shrilled. "Oh my God." She smacked kisses on his lips. "You realize what this is?" she whispered, smiling.

"What? That you're crazy?" Fuck, what was she doing to him?

"No! That *you're crazy! About me!*" she busted out laughing, and Sade grinned.

"Finally, something I can agree with. I am crazy about you." He rolled onto her and kissed her lips, liking that he could even if it did nothing for his sadomasochistic needs. "Might not be the kind of crazy you're thinking."

She moaned softly under his worship of her mouth. "What kind?"

"The kind of crazy that isn't nice. The kind that likes to tie you up and make you suffer pleasure. Maybe pain." Sade's dick got hard and she gasped.

"I felt that," she whispered.

Like a flickering light bulb, it left as quickly as it'd come with her excitement.

"I think the key is to *not* want it," he said, kissing her again, softer. "Wanting it to come sends it away."

She stroked along his scalp with soft fingers. "You… seem not upset?"

"Until I am."

"A timetable." She smiled against his lips, her hands roaming his back and bare ass now. "What if I… try a few things?"

He groaned. "In the basement?"

She gasped again when his dick throbbed then hissed in displeasure. "I hate that place."

His hard on slowly left.

"But I'm willing to try! Geeze you're so sensitive."

He paused. "You think this is me deciding this? If it were me, I'd have my cock buried in you right now, fucking you so hard that you screamed until you were hoarse."

She gave a light gasp.

"Yeah exactly." He rolled off of her and put an arm over his face.

She turned to him. "How about... we mix it up a little? A little pain, a little emotion?"

"A little oil? A little water?"

"I'm willing to try if you're willing. What do you have to lose?"

"Nothing," he muttered. Except her. When she was tired of him never being normal.

****

"I think... it's safe to say that I am very turned on with giving you an orgasm," he confessed, staring at her tied wide open on the table..

She mumbled something behind her gag, followed by more emphatic mumbling that sucked the desire from him. He walked over and pulled the gag out. "Sorry," she gasped, looking toward him in her blindfold. "I was just saying no pain no gain and then realized you might think I was needing to say something and so was… trying to tell you never mind just go on."

"Only I don't speak mm-mm-m-mmm."

She bit her lip trying not to smile. "Right. My bad."

"Are you comfortable?" he asked.

"Not at all," she said. "Is that… do you like that?"

"In this second, yes. That could change in the next."

"I'll try harder to be a good student. Would you like me to call you anything? Like sir, or master? Teacher maybe?"

Fuck she was too adorable for this shit.

"What? Am I talking too much?"

"No, Mercy, you're being you too much."

She bit her lip. "Tell me how to be, I'm a good actress."

"But I'll know you're acting."

"So? Come on, just try, you may discover an exception to your rules or a loophole. Oh God," she gasped.

"What," he said, concerned.

"My ass. I think it's cramping."

Sade rolled his eyes and undid her.

"Why are you undoing me? It'll pass!"

"This isn't going to work, not now at least."

"You barely tried!"

"I know it won't, I'm not in the mood."

She gave annoyed huffs. "Then let's try you. Let me try arousing you. I'll tie you up."

Only because he didn't want her too discouraged. "Fine. I'll try."

"Yes!" she said, eagerly, removing the blindfold once he freed her hands. Sade sat on the bed she was tied to and she climbed in his lap, wrapping her arms around his neck."

"Foreplay. Nice." Despite his effort to be sarcastic, he returned her hug, his body waking to that new addiction—her. Jaded yet innocent. An angel with a broken wing, patched together with sheer determination to survive and live and be… so fucking beautiful.

"Okay, let's get to it!" She hopped off his lap and looked around.

Sade watched her, that heat all in his chest again, wondering how the fuck he ended up where he was. At what exact point did he go from watching the magic act from the audience, to volunteering to be cut in half by the beautiful magician.

"Oh, what about we try your board thing?"

He quirked a brow at her. "Only if you plan on using it right."

She bit her lip. "I can just… try a few things. If it works, great, if not, well we tried."

He lowered his head and spread his arms wide. "Test subject ready."

She clapped happily and Sade was sure he would be content to try all day with her if it didn't mean leading her closer and closer to discouragement. Once she got him restrained, she brought the blindfold.

"No," he said.

"Why?"

"The blindfold takes me… to dark places."

"Oh," she said, tossing it quickly, like she definitely didn't want him going to dark places. "Don't need that. Eyelids work just as good if you need to not see."

Sade watched her, studied her, that heat in his chest unbearable now. He also noted then that she always kept her breasts covered with one or both forearms. He also realized that his body didn't find her humiliation or intimidation arousing. Let the sexual complications pile up.

Mercy went through several items on a wall and pulled down a flogger. "Not using metal," she said, glancing at him.

"My dick will have to give you the heads up. Pun intended. But, we're trying, I remember."

She walked over with it and stood before him. "Right. Now, where should I start?"

"Wherever you'd like."

She nodded and took a few breaths. "Okay." She waved the flogger around a few times, then tested the striking distance of the light straps to the right. She eyed him. "Are you ready?"

"Dying with anticipation."

She finally launched her first strike. "Did that hurt?"

"Fucking horrific. Death by noodle beatings."

"Okay, okay," she said in light determination. "Warming up the arm."

She swung again, and his cock jerked with the sting.

"Ohhh, nice," she whispered, seeing it. She struck again.

This time the sting shot desire through him. "Yes," he whispered.

"Yes?" she eyed his growing cock and swung again.

"Yes, do it," he urged. "Faster."

She began really flogging him and he growled under the mix of pain and desire, wishing he had on his choking gear.

Sade gasped when her mouth was suddenly on his cock, sucking eagerly. Jesus Christ. "Fucking use your teeth," he gushed, looking down.

She scraped them along his cock and he pumped his hips. "Deeper, take it deep."

She did exactly that and then pressed her hand onto his abs. Her nails dug a little and he gasped. "Break the skin, Mercy!"

The pain of her nails raking down his stomach was countered by her worried whimpers. Not enough to cancel it out but enough to piss him off. "Fucking do it Mercy!"

The tides turned against him when she placed kisses all along the length of his cock. The adoration brought that heat to his chest, which in turn slowly turned his cock limp.

She struggled valiantly to revive his stupid dick, the sheer effort making him softer with each second. "I'm sorry," he whispered, winded with that other need now. "I need to feel you against me."

She quickly stood and pressed her body into his, hugging him. "It's okay," she whispered. "It was a good try. You did so good," she praised, making him clench his eyes tight with that stabbing need that stole his breath. He didn't know that feeling, he just knew that is was fucking exhilarating and terrifying at the same time, like falling from a cliff in the dark.

She kissed him and more of the same flooded him. At least it liked kissing. In fact, it seemed to like anything he didn't like before. "I need to taste you," he whispered.

"You like tasting me?" she nibbled at his lip and some of that fire went down below at the hint of naughty in her tone.

"I do."

"I can make you, if you want."

"Oh fuck," he whispered, his cock bursting to life. "Yes. Yes, that."

"Where do you want it?"

"You tell me. Make me."

She unstrapped him and pointed to the bed table. "Go there. No wait," she said, making him pause. "Your bed. I have a surprise."

Sade walked over and pulled her into his arms, kissing her, embracing that other power. The Mercy Power. That's what it was. Raining down on him, a torrent of raw heat. "I'm going to make you scream my name," he growled.

She went a little limp in his arms and he smiled, liking the effect. He lifted her by her ass and put her on his waist, heading to his bedroom with her. She giggled the entire way, kissing him all over his face. "I like you carrying me."

"Do you?" he whispered, kicking his door open. He got to the bed and crawled with her to the center and laid her down.

"Oh," she said. "My surprise." She pushed him onto his back and got up on her elbow smiling at him. "You better get ready. I'm going to rock your world."

He couldn't resist his laughter at how adorable that was coming from a sweet angel. And how true. "You better hurry, I'm holding my breath."

She scrambled off the bed, leaving Sade alone with his feelings and thoughts. He wouldn't over think it, not now. Later maybe. Right now he'd do just what he said and enjoy the fuck out of it.

"Close your eyes," she called from the hallway.

Jesus, would her angelic qualities never end? She was every bit a little girl in her heart still. It made Sade want to kill anything that might threaten that. "Closed."

"Aaaand open."

He smiled at the eager pride in her voice, but at seeing her in that pure white teddy skyrocketed his need to pleasure her.

"You don't like it?" she worried.

His eyes raised to hers and he shook his head. "I never said that."

"Oh…" She bit her lower lip and eyed his straining cock, getting exactly what he thought of it. "Oh," she gasped.

"Hurry Miss Mercy before I take without permission."

Her arousal with that threat woke more *new* needs in him he'd not had before. He usually liked taking control to give pleasure with pain, never just pleasure. Sade sat up slowly, already knowing. He would make good on that threat now.

"Sade," she gasped, watching him carefully. "I thought I was…"

"Changed my mind."

"To… what?"

"I think you know."

She let out several breaths and slowly walked in reverse until the wall was at her back.

"I want you on this bed," he said walking slowly toward her. "I want you on your stomach. I want those pretty legs wide open. I want your tight fucking ass lifted high… so I can suck you… suck you right to the brink of orgasm." Sade pressed his hard cock into her stomach. "I want to punish you Mercy. With unbearable pleasure. I want to make you suffer with it. While you scream my name. My name Mercy. I want my name to be the only name you ever scream." And he really hoped his cock would let him fuck her. He fucking wanted to know what that felt like with her more than ever now.

Chapter Seventeen

Mercy ran to the bed, ready to have him. She laid on the center but didn't open her legs. She kept them tightly shut. She'd never experienced such desire as she did when he'd tied her up and made her. She liked it. Very much she realized. And the idea of him making her while not tied was… God yes.

She felt him get on the bed from the foot. "Naughty Mercy," he muttered. He took hold of her ankles and spread her wide. She resisted him, liking very much the feel of his strong hands making her. For pleasure. It was all for pleasure and it made her feel safe. He made her feel safe. No matter how mean he sounded, how scary he behaved or looked, she'd never felt safer with anybody.

She gave a yelp when he spanked her butt. "Lift it."

She obeyed with desperate moans, her limbs trembling as she gripped the covers tight. She gasped when he ripped the material off of her and slid his finger along her folds. "Mmmm. Somebody is a naughty girl." She heard him lick his finger before teasing at her down there again.

She panted and grunted for his touch, even moved her hips. "Yes." His strong fingers wrapped her upper thighs as he pressed his thumbs at her entrance.

"Mercy..." he slid his finger slowly in, always gentle and careful with her. She flicked her hips, liking when he did it in and out really fast.

"Do it," she cried.

He bit her butt and she jumped with a gasp. He gave a low moan and a shudder took her. She lifted higher, wanting more. He spanked her ass none too softly then slid his palm gently over the spot. His other finger moved slowly in and out of her. He spanked again, the force more than a small sting but still only enough to send fire shooting to her privates and her heart racing. She loved the feel of his power on her body. So exactly controlled for her.

"Sade," she begged. "Make love to me."

His finger slowed for a bit then finally slid out of her. She lifted up and turned to see him kneeling behind her, his head lowered and his eyes clenched tight.

"I'm sorry," she whispered, confused. Was it the love word?

He shook his head a little. "It's not you."

She sat up now, pulling her knees to her chest, watching him. "It's okay, we can stop. Try again later," she said, trying to sound unbothered.

He sat down at the foot of the bed, his back to her. Mercy crawled over, worried now. What if he got tired of her always making him try things he failed at? What if he got tired of her period? She sat next to him in the same position as he was. "Big girl panties," she said.

He angled a look at her.

"That's what I was chanting the other day. I do it when I'm scared." She shoved his shoulder lightly with hers. "Hey, I got leftover lasagna if you're hungry?"

"Why?"

"Because... you never finished it."

"I mean, why Mercy," he whispered, shaking his lowered head.

Her heart raced. "Why what?"

He continued shaking it for several moments then looked at her, his eyes burning and raw. "Why are you here?"

She swallowed at the confusion in his tone, the questioning.

"Why me? Why did you pick me? The fucked up one? The shattered in a million pieces one?"

The *to help you* mantra sounded like a gimmick in her own ears and she held them back.

He got up and paced now. "Why me, Mercy? Did you have a dream? What made you choose me? Why did you really go down that alley? Did God tell you to? Did he send you?"

Fear and confusion made her head swim. He seemed so sincere, so desperate for that to be the case. And here, the real case was withheld from him. More panic hit her at realizing what would happen if he ever found out. It would shatter his ability to trust anything she said. "Sade," she gasped. "I… I need to tell you something."

His expression slowly sobered to a look of doom, like he'd expected bad to come and here it was.

"Listen to me," she hurried. "I didn't tell you this because I didn't want to sound like… a stalker." When he merely stared silently, she hurried on. "I was in that alley to look for you because I knew you. My father was a good man, he liked to help people. And… two weeks after he passed away, I found an envelope at my house. And when I opened it… there you were."

Sade suddenly turned and covered his face with both hands a moment. "Wow!" He let out several gasps. "You fucking lied to me!"

At hearing the zero tolerance tone, she shot up from the bed. "I'm sorry! Sade, I-I was scared, you had me tied up. I didn't know what you'd think if I told you about the envelope. You already thought I was a detective, please believe me."

He mumbled things she couldn't make out, then spun to her. "Who the fuck is your father, Mercy?"

"Kurt Larson. He was just a good man, he liked helping people down and out, like he did with me."

"And you thought my report hit your door because what? A charity case?"

At hearing how absurd that sounded, she said, "See? See how hard that is to believe? That's why I didn't tell you."

"Mercy," he said, his eyes boring into hers. "It's not only hard to believe it's *obviously* so fucking wrong!" He paced now. "How did you say your father died? Can you believe I was stupid enough not to check all this shit out?"

"No, no, no, my father was a nobody, he had a landscaping business. He-he was a true man of God. This is a fact, the solid truth." She pounded each statement with a fist in her palm.

He looked at her for a long time, like something becoming clear to him.

"Sade please," she gasped, tears falling now. "I mean it, he was just a good man and I was just trying to carry on that goodness, I promise," she whispered. "I was trying to give him something back, he sacrificed so much and I thought, I thought when I saw your file, what else could it be for but to help you? And so I went to find you and-and meet you, just to see what I might be able to do and you know the story from there, that's it!"

He paced again, holding his head. "I need to fucking call Mordecai."

"Who is that?" She followed him out the room.

"Somebody who knows everything." Mercy covered her top with her hands, trembling. Sade eyed her. "Get dressed."

Pain sledge-hammered her chest at his angry tone while telling her that. She felt dirty and stupid as she hurried out before she gave in to the sobs clawing at her throat. In a daze she dressed in jeans and a t-shirt. She jumped when he appeared at her door.

"What's your father's name again?" She gave it but her voice didn't carry. "I can't fucking hear you!"

"Kurt Larson," she barely said louder, trembling everywhere now.

He repeated the name in the phone and Mercy sat on the bed, panic slowly building in her. Something bad was coming. Something so bad. Something so painful she wouldn't survive it.

She couldn't handle that. She had to get away. She couldn't face what was coming, not from, him.

Mercy quietly got her purse and waited till he was out of sight before she slipped out. Choking back sobs, she ran to her car and got in, fighting with the keys as the wails escaped her. Yanking on her seat belt, she screamed with the pounding on her window, shoving the keys into ignition.

"Mercy!" he yelled. "Open the door!"

No, no, no. She couldn't. She couldn't hear the words, not one more cutting word. Not from him. Anybody but him.

In blinding agony, she tore out of the driveway and screamed when he ran and beat on her trunk. She stepped on the accelerator, glancing over her shoulder. It was seeing him naked in the road that distracted her for one too many seconds. She jerked her head forward in time to see the tree just before her. She hit the brakes only to find she had none. Yanking the wheel right, she clipped the tree with the corner of the vehicle. Mercy screamed as the world spun with the flipping car. She held on tight to the steering wheel. *God please. Please help me.*

****

Terror gripped Sade at the nightmare before him. He ran with all he had to Mercy's car, now upside down. He reached it and found Mercy dangling from her seat belt, unconscious while Sade fought to open her door. Fuck, God, no. He raced to the passenger side and yanked it open.

"Mercy," he gasped, looking along her body. How hurt was she?

She moaned suddenly.

"Mercy, can you hear me? Wake up baby!" Sade said.

"Sade," she barely managed.

"What hurts angel? I need to know." He climbed out of the car and looked around. "Help me!" he roared. "Call 911!"

He climbed back in the car.

"I'm… I'm stuck," she mumbled. "I can't get out!"

"Just be still. I need to call an ambulance, okay?"

"I'm fine, I'm just…" she looked around. "What's wrong?" she asked. She looked forward. "I hit a tree. My brakes didn't work."

No brakes? Fear slammed him at what that could mean. "Yes, you hit a tree," he said. "No, don't try to move! Don't try to… Mercy please stop, don't move!"

"I'm fine, I'm just stuck."

Sade smelled gas and quickly unbuckled her and pulled her out of the car. Where the fuck was everybody? How late was it?

Sade carried her all the way back to the condo and kicked the door shut then hurried to lay her on the couch.

"My head hurts," she whispered.

"Fuck," he gasped at seeing her finally. She was banged up. Air bag burns on her face and chest. Bruises already forming on her arms. Sade collapsed to his knees next to her. "I'm so fucking sorry," he gasped, laying his head on her chest. "I shouldn't have talked to you that way, baby, I'm so sorry."

Her hands cradled his head and she shhhh'd him. "Sokay," she whispered. "I'm sorry too. For lying. I told you the truth because…"

He raised his head when she didn't go on and found her fighting back a sob.

"Because I was afraid you'd find out and not ever trust me," she choked out. "And I wanted you to trust me, I wanted you to feel safe with me," she wailed.

"I know I'm safe with you angel. I know that," he whispered, kissing her forehead. He may have been pissed about the lie but he didn't think she had a single bad bone in her body, that much he was sure of.

"It would kill me," she wailed. "I can't take you hating me, I can't. I'd rather die, Sade."

"I don't hate you. I could never hate you." he whispered, his chest unbearably tight as he pressed kisses to her face. "I don't hate you."

The phone rang. "Don't move," he said, "I'll be right back." He hoped it was Mordecai with answers.

Sade ran to the kitchen. "What you got for me?"

He opened up with a sigh. "Man. It's not good."

Sade's heart hammered. "Just tell me." He was ready to hit whatever it was head on.

"I've got a few more things to double check but I think you might be dating the daughter of Kane fucking Kross man."

Terror slammed Sade. "What!? No, no, her father is dead, and, no, that's not her fucking father anyway." Sade's head spun with gory KK images. "Fuck, since when does he have a *daughter*?"

"Since we found out. Recently," he whispered like he worried they might be heard. "And he is *not* dead my friend. She no doubt believes he is, though."

Sade leaned against the wall, closing his eyes. "Why would she? Why would she believe he's dead?" Fear was stealing his ability to breathe, much less string thoughts together. KK. Anybody but that man.

"Because I think he needed to be dead and when you need to be dead, nobody knows."

"Why would you think it's him? No, that is not his daughter, sorry man but she doesn't match."

"She wouldn't know, Sade," he hissed incredulously. "You think he'd tell her? High-fucking-un-likely. Hey baby doll, daddy's gotta run out and castrate a few bad guys, don't wait up? And that was the other thing I wanted to tell you."

"Oh fuck." Mordecai's tone said he wouldn't like this.

"Your father has gotten wind of her snooping around. He had me check her out."

"Oh God, fuck, you told him all this?"

"Do I *work* for him? I'm telling you as a heads up. If you're still seeing her, I'd watch her back. And yours for stray bullets."

Sade fought to piece everything together. "And why do you think her dad isn't dead?"

"Because three people died just in the last week."

"Our team?"

"Yep. All assigned to get an angle on your girl."

Sade put his hand on his mouth. "Fffuuuuck, I can't believe this. Who all knows?"

"Everybody but you."

"And why the fuck?"

"You *know* why. The only reason I'm telling you now is because you just gave me what I've been wondering."

"And what's that?"

Sade waited in the sudden silence before he finally mumbled, "Where your head was with her."

"Oh yeah? And where is it?"

"Nowhere I'm afraid. You're all heart in this one dude. And I've got one bit of advice for you."

"I'm listening." Sade paced in the silence, waiting.

"Run. Run far and run fast."

Sade didn't say another word, he just hung up and looked around for glowing red crosshairs in the shape of a crucifix. Ffffuuuuck. Her father was fucking Kane Kross? As a boy, Sade had secretly idolized the communities archenemy. Sade had gotten his own nickname early on as a challenge to the Vigilante who seemed to specialize in killing bad guys. Nobody knew that Sade had a secret death wish, and to be killed by the Vigilante would have been his dream come true, the final bucket list item. But when he grew up, Sade had changed his mind about how he would die. He taunted death a lot like it taunted him. And if he ever got considered by the elite assassin, he was ready. Except not like this. Especially with Mercy, because he felt it in the blood rushing through his veins in that second that Mercy was *his*. And he needed to be fucking alive for that.

So who were they running from exactly? KK or his father? Any man would rather be hunted by his father than by KK. Sade would be running from both in this case.

He realized one thing and quickly dialed Mordecai back. "What if it's not him, it could be anybody. Somebody her father left to look after her?"

"If it is, he left them with his signature."

Sade closed his eyes and hung up the phone. Fuck. KK killed all his victims with bullets cast in a shell bearing a crucifix. And in case you didn't get the message with that, he left it on the body, bullet holes along the abdomen in the same shape. But maybe the most fearsome thing he did was brand the balls of every man with that image. After he sawed off their dick and shoved them in the ass or mouth of the owner.

Now God's avenging angel would come. Ten years too fucking late, when he didn't *want shit* to do with him.

Chapter Eighteen

Sade paced in the living room while Mercy rested. The doorbell rang and he ran to it with his gun and glanced into the peephole. Bo. He opened the door and yanked him in and put a finger to his lips.

"You need to leave now!" Bo mouthed.

"What?" Sade whispered. "Why didn't you *call*!" Sade raced to his bedroom with Bo on his heels.

"They have my phone tapped man, couldn't risk it!"

"Did you fucking hear?" Sade said quietly, yanking a black bag out of his closet. "About fucking KK?"

"Yes man, I did! I'm not supposed to tell you but I had to." he whispered. "They're going to hurt her man."

Sade eyed him briefly, shaking his head. "I need to get her out of here before that happens."

"They want to bring her in now that they know man, you need to hurry."

"Fuck!" Sade gasped, pointing at him. "Not a word to her about this being her dad, do you hear me?" He nodded and Sade ran to the vault and got enough cash for a year and several firearms, then hurried to Mercy's room.

He shook her and she bolted up in bed. "What!"

"Listen to me." He pulled her up from the bed and caressed her face between his hands. "You're in danger here."

"What? Why?"

"I don't have time to explain everything you'll have to trust me, can you do that Mercy? Can you baby? Trust me?"

She nodded, her eyes darting to Bo then back to Sade.

"Now listen closely. You listening?" He made her look in his eyes. "I'm going to give you a key, an address, a bag of money and a few weapons. You're going to zigzag your way to this address. It's four hours north of here and nobody knows about this place but me. Are you listening Mercy," he hissed, when she clenched her eyes shut.

"Yes, I'm listening," she wiped her tears away. "Tell me what to do, I'll do it."

He put a set of keys in her hand and closed it tight around them. "These are the keys to the place, and there's an antique truck in the parking garage. It's ready to move. Once you get in it, you do not stop, you do not make a phone call. In fact, leave your phone here. If you have an emergency of any kind, use a payphone and call the police. Not me." He took her hand now and began tugging her to the door. "I have enough money in this bag, a couple of firearms and extra ammunition should you need it for anything. When you get there, you don't move. Don't lift your head. Just hide. I'll come as soon as the coast is clear."

They all made a dash to the private parking garage and Sade led her to the truck. He looked around and unlocked the door then helped her in, making sure she knew how to drive a stick shift. She wiped her tears and nodded, assuring him she understood.

Sade pulled her face to his and meshed their lips with a near panic. "There's a map in the glove box. Do not stop," he whispered. "Do you fucking understand me? I swear to God, you better not stop, I mean it Mercy. Swear on your father you will not stop."

She nodded. "I promise, I swear," she gasped.

He kissed her once more in the same way and put his forehead to hers. "No matter what happens angel..." He looked into her gaze for several seconds, breathing hard around the emotions. "I..." Fuck. He closed his eyes and cleared his throat before opening them and soul meshing hard with her. "You're *my* Mercy. My fucking Mercy, there is *no* other woman in this fucking world..." he whispered, "that I ever want to know. The way I know you." He stroked her face between his hands and kissed her hard again.

"Sade!" she cried quietly, shaking her head. "Where are you going? Just come with me," she gasped. "Please don't stay, please come."

"I've gotta make a deal with my father that he can't refuse. But there are no guarantees in this fucking life. Look at me, Mercy. We're survivors. No matter what happens, right?"

She choked out a sob and nodded. "Okay okay," she whispered, stroking his face. "So I'll see you tonight?"

"More like tomorrow night." He turned to Bo and aimed a finger at him. "You want out of this, you leave now. Run. But if you stay, nobody fucking hurts Mercy, do you understand?" Sade gripped his shoulder and shook it. "Do you fucking understand me? If you want out brother, take it now! Haul ass to the end of the earth and don't look back, I don't care. But if you stay?" Sade pointed in his face and grit his teeth. "You better be ready to have your dick cut off and shoved in your ass, because if you're with me, you're a shield for her."

Bo nodded. "Yeah man, I'm a shield. I'm staying with you man. I'm a shield."

Sade turned to Mercy and pulled her face to his again for one last kiss before pressing his mouth to her ear and gave her the address then whispered, *big girl panties baby*."

He shut her door and ran to hide where he could watch the road after her. Nobody knew that vehicle was his. Nobody. He'd bought it years ago for when he would make his break next year. Everything he did for that event was under new identities. She'd be safe at least. While he went to strike a deal with his fucking father, the devil.

****

"623 Fallen LN Prairie City, Oregon," she wailed quietly, "623 Fallen LN, Prairie City, Oregon." Mercy wiped her eyes again and drove slowly out of Los Angeles, feeling like a neon sign in the robin egg blue truck. Keeping her eyes peeled for anybody following her, fear kept her stomach in tight knots for the entire hour it took to get far enough out of town to breathe. "Please God," she gasped. "Please help us. Help Sade. Watch over him, I beg you."

Mercy stopped a few times within the next two hours to read the map and make sure she wasn't too far off track of her zigzagging. She was not far now. She'd passed the location up on purpose. Sade would be impressed with that when she told him.

She drove fifteen mph down the final road looking for the turn that should be there. Was it gravel? Dirt? She was in the middle of nowhere land. Good thing she had no issues with horror movie scenarios playing out in her head right at that moment.

"Big girl panties Mercy, big girl panties." She hit the brake when she passed a narrow road. Putting the truck in reverse, she backed up and stared at it. "Geeze, that's not the least bit scary." But that had to be it. Even though there were no visible signs that anything would be at the end of the road but Big Foot or something worse. A psycho in the woods.

She turned onto the narrow lane, big enough for one vehicle and wound her way up a hill. Two miles later and she was looking for a spot to turn around. Nothing could be this far up. And if it was, she didn't want to arrive alone. The place was fucking creepy. She loved nature and everything but this was way too horror movie for her.

"Oh my God!" she gasped at finally spotting white through the trees ahead. A few more seconds and she came to a stop before a white shingle cottage on the side of a mountain. "Wow," she whispered. Gorgeous. She looked around and shivered at the ideas of what lived in these untouched woods. She wasn't really wanting to use her Wing-Chun on a bear or a mountain lion.

Fifteen minutes later, she worked up the nerve to get out of the truck. *We're gonna run to the door and zip in.* She gave another careful look into the darkness all around. *Run in and lock, run in and lock.* Shit, what about spiders along the way?

She searched the truck for a flashlight. Nothing. Damn. She could leave the headlights on. She'd have to. Find a flashlight inside and come back out. Or find exterior lights.

A howl nearby made her jump and she scanned the dark. Shit! Shit! Putting on any exterior lights might ward off animals. While telling the neighborhood psycho somebody was home.

Mercy took several breaths and grabbed the duffle bag and her purse and looped them across her body. *Big girl panties.* She opened the door, jumped out, and ran to the front of the house, slowing a bit at the steps to make sure she wasn't running headlong into a huge spider web. Fuck, she hated spiders *bad!*

She shuddered the rest of the way onto the porch, eyes taking in everything as she went. The outside furniture had sharp angles, maybe wood. She eyed the four body sized, break and enter windows along the front as she fought the key into the deadbolt. Panic hit her suddenly. What if this wasn't the right house? What if there was an alarm when she tried to open the door? *Shit*. She looked around for an address on the place. Nothing of course. She didn't recall even a damn mailbox anywhere along the way.

She held her breath and turned the key in the lock then jolted when the metal released with an ominous clonk. She darted a glance over her shoulder at feeling like something had crept up behind her. She quickly opened the door and slipped inside, her hand trembling along the wood surface for the fucking lock. She finally located it and turned it quickly.

She looked around now, feeling like she'd just graduated to Hell part two. But the key worked. This had to be the right place.

Hunched at the door, she looked around in the dark, allowing her eyes to adjust before she moved an inch. Her nose picked up cedar... pine... vanilla? Maybe cinnamon. Her ears picked up zero as the shadows slowly came into view. She soon made out the shape of furniture then suddenly froze. Somebody stood in the fucking corner. Oh God. She held her breath and waited, not moving.

Ah shit. She let out a breath. It was just a viney looking tree. Jesus what a stupid thing to have right there. Her breath trembled in and out as she gazed around. Living room, kitchen, dining. She made out stair rails along the far end of the wall. So that meant the dormer windows above weren't just decoration. A story and a half home. Small but well laid out.

She spied two doors to the right of the living room. Probably a bathroom and laundry. Or a bedroom. She wanted to turn on lights but wasn't ready to be seen. God, she still needed to go back out and lock the truck and turn off the lights before the battery ran down. Last thing she needed was to be stranded.

Her night vision kicked in more and she looked around for a small lamp or something. Spying one on the table to her right, she made her way slowly to it, feeling along the base. The light flickered on by touch, startling her. Darting a quick look around, she tapped the base until it dimmed to the lowest setting.

She glanced at the windows. Heavily draped and shut tight. Thank you God. She made her way to a fireplace between the doors on the right wall to see the pictures on the mantle. As she drew closer, she realized they weren't just empty frames. She snatched the first one off and angled it toward the light, making out a woman and a young boy, smiling at the camera. Mercy's heart jerked hard with a gasp at recognizing Sade's features in the tiny adorable Superman costume. Dear God, he couldn't have been more than five. Her vision blurred and she quickly wiped her eyes, looking at the woman. His mother? Oh God they looked…so happy together. What had happened to her?

Her heart constricted at how *beautiful* she was. Just how did she end up in that life? Was she forced like she'd been? Trapped into it? Mercy wished she'd dug more now to find out details about her death. She'd planned on it and got caught up in helping Sade.

She stroked the picture, realizing. Maybe this was the path she'd been seeking that led to the heart of his wounds. This right here.

Mercy set it back down carefully and looked at the other pictures. Who were these couples and families? She looked closer and realized they were the generic photos that came with the frames. Pain hammered her heart at why they were still in them. Was that the only photo he had of his mother? Was this his attempt at a normal life? She looked all around then, finding a home that seemed well lived in. Was this a long lost family home? No, he said nobody knew about it.

He had one more year to work for his father, then he was free. She slid her hands over the books on a bookshelf. Was this his freedom? This place? This new life? A sob tore from her chest for him. He better fucking make it back here. He better! She covered her hand over her mouth, allowing herself to think of what he was doing at that moment. She closed her eyes tight and prayed for him again. *God please, please, bring him back safe to me.*

Mercy looked around and noticed a clock. If it was right, it was four in the morning. She made her way around the home finding she was right about what was behind the doors next to the fireplace. She covered her mouth at entering the downstairs bedroom. A superhero themed bedroom sat in perfect order. Had he lived here once maybe? She swallowed hard and checked every corner and closet, mostly to make sure they were empty, her mind processing everything it touched. Were these his toys? She glided her fingers over them, feeling so much love that it made her sob. She bet he was such a sweet little boy at that age.

She looked around, imagining him playing there. It was so easy to do.

Still not turning on any more lights, she finally climbed the stairs and stood at the foot of a short hall. Faint moonlight streamed in from a window at the end of the hall. She noticed doors on the left and right of it as she walked to peer out. She stared down into the darkness below, unable to make out much of the shadows.

She turned to the door on the right and opened it. A bathroom. She explored it enough to make sure it was empty then found another dormer window along the wall near the toilet. It was smaller than the hall one and again she peered down into shadows.

She looked around the bathroom and found more items that said it had been lived in. A woman's items. His mother? Thoughts of it being someone else made her stomach sick. She hurried out to the final door and found the master bedroom as she'd expected. The décor was very feminine. Lots of white lace and tiny flowers. Mercy burned with questions. The walk in closet turned out empty. Odd. In the room itself, she found a few items on the dresser—a jewelry box. Hair brush. She opened the jewelry box. Empty. She picked up the brush and pulled at the bristles, coming away with nothing.

She glanced around, ready to explore downstairs a little better. She needed to keep her mind occupied until daylight. Shit, the lights on the truck!

Mercy headed downstairs to the kitchen and searched for a flashlight. At finding one in a pantry, she made the mad freaky dash to the truck, locked it up, and raced back inside.

Mercy's breath froze then at hearing muted ringing. A phone? She jerked around listening and quickly searched, still afraid to turn on lights. Where was it coming from?

Chapter Nineteen

"You don't need to come in." Sade got out of his car.

"I'm coming man. I'm with you in this," Bo said.

"You realize how this can end? Do you?" Sade eyed him as he headed toward the backside of the club leading to the meeting room where his father waited for him *all ears* concerning Sade's mention of a proposition.

"I know man, trust me," Bo said. "How long have we known each other? You had my back all my life, I'm here to the end."

Guilt hit Sade. He didn't even like Bo on any reasonable level. He was just a part of his life like a stop sign was part of the road. And yet you'd swear Sade had been such an amazing friend to him. Sade got a small glimpse of himself in that moment—who he was, what he'd become over the years. A cold, walled off human, unable to see outside his own bullshit.

Until Mercy. She'd wiggled her way beyond his barricade. Slipped right in. And for the first time in his life, since his mother, he felt alive. The kind of alive you feel when you walk out into the sun and it soaks deep into your bones, and fills you with hopes and dreams that are not impossible. And the idea that anything would dare threaten that rare fucking beauty again, brought out the vilest of his sadism. He was only four the last time that happened, unable to do a fucking thing but embrace the monster it made him. But now… now his father wasn't pushing around a four year old. He was pushing around the freak he'd made. Now Sade took life like he took a breath. Without thought or care. But he needed to think now. He needed to be smart not just lethal. There was no room for fucking up.

Sade ignored the demons in his head that had gathered against him, whispering and mockingly wondering if Sade could do anything without fucking it up. And now he had Bo with him and it suddenly seemed all wrong. He turned in the hall just outside his father's office and stopped him. "Just leave, Bo. You don't need to fucking be here."

The hurt look on his face confused Sade. Where did Bo get this loyalty? Why did he have it? "Man," he said, offended. "I'm here. I'm here for you."

"Why? I've not been there for you, just leave!"

He shook his head. "You're wrong, you've been there. Not up my ass but there. A shadow in my life but a strong one." He shook his head. "You're my family even if you ain't really. I can't be picky, you know?"

The desperation in Bo to have the very thing Sade was fighting for, hit him hard. "Listen Bo. If we don't live past today, you need to know…" Sade locked eyes with him and grabbed the back of his head and put his forehead to his. "I'm sorry. I should have been better to you, okay?"

"We're not angels, man?" he chuckled softly. "That's your Mercy. She's worth it. And I wanna be with you in this, let me be with you."

Sade nodded, vaguely remembering that desperate feeling of needing to belong to somebody, be with somebody. "I'll do all the talking."

"Right behind you man."

Sade made a mental note to get to know Bo as an actual person if they lived through this. He had a lot to make up with him.

The door opened after Sade's code knock and in silence, they both walked in and the first thing he noticed was the new face. A man he didn't recognize sat in one of the chairs before his father's opulent desk in his opulent office.

"The prodigal son has returned," his father boomed as he stood with arms open wide. His Brooklyn accent seemed to grow thicker each year despite several decades and a thousand mile divide from his roots. Or maybe it just sounded thicker to Sade since he hated it, hated him. His aging fingers glittered with gold and diamonds, all paid for by stolen innocence in the form of blood, sex, and tears. But then what Sade bought to the table wasn't much better. It wasn't flesh trade, he'd drawn hard limits with the sick fuck on that front, but many of the men Sade fought and often killed weren't exactly deserving of the death they got.

"Sit down my good and faithful son. Bo, how are you? How's business?"

"Good Mr. Ashcroft."

Sade and Bo sat when his father did, as per his stupid custom. Sade had been taking notes on the new face. He wasn't from around there, he was sure. The other three on duty he knew but this new guy carried a dangerous vibe. Sleek, well-dressed, well-built said professional killer. The gleam in his near black and penetrating gaze said heartless. Very bad combination.

"Son," his father began in an offended tone. "You never told me you were *dating*. I mean I'm heartbroken to think you would not introduce me."

"If you leave her alone, I'll work for you another twenty years. I'll even take over the arms division and make you more money than you can ever count." You dumb fuck.

"Wow!" his father said, slapping his hand on the desk. "That's a *beautiful* offer. Irresistible. But… I have a little bit of a problem, see. I'm sorry, I forgot to introduce you to Mr. Buckles." His father held a hand to the man. "See, he's here right now, ready to give daddy two million dollars, and for what?" He shrugged his shoulders. "Not to hurt her, but just to have a few words with her."

Sade's heart hammered. This was it. Where things got very fucking shitty. Just exactly how and to what degree was the question.

"To talk?" he looked at *Mr. Buckles.* "About what? Maybe I can answer your questions."

The man only laughed softly with his crossed legs. "I must see her. She is... very important to me."

"Why?" Sade asked, unable to bite his tongue or smooth his tone.

"Why? Simple," the man said, uncrossing his legs and sitting straight. "I want to use her for bait. It's her father that I want most of all."

"Who doesn't?" Sade's father boomed. "That piece of shit has all but ruined my empire! See... son. This is business, and you know my motto. Business before family. When I learned who your girlfriend was, I was heartbroken for you," he lied smoothly. "So much potential that one. And *talent.* Before I decided to sell her out to Mr. Buckles here, I had actually considered offering her a job with the family. So we could all work together."

The reality of what Sade had done by allowing Mercy into his life hit him hard. What started as a cute little cat and mouse sexual game had gone very fucking wrong. This was it. The fork in the road. "I won't sell her out. Not even if you torture me. And I think you know that."

"Torture! Would I ever do that?" his father declared, an offended hand on his chest. "Torture my own son? Do I look like a heartless man? Now, Mr. Buckles here on the other hand is quite fluent in the business of slow or sudden heart cessations. He's here in fact, to help accomplish this business transaction that *is* happening with or without your cooperation."

"Can't get information from a dead man, daddy," Sade muttered.

His father stared at him, shaking his head. "Always the difficult son." He stood and opened his drawer, pulling out his stash of cigars and offering one to Mr. Buckles who waved him off. He lit it and squinted his eye at Sade then turned to the man. "He's always been a handful, always difficult. Did you know he got his own mother killed?"

Sade held his jaw shut tight.

"He was a momma's boy, always has been. Don't know what the fuck she saw in that little shit or what kind of spell he put on her, but she was one of my *best* whores until that little fucker right there," he pointed at Sade. "I tried to be nice. I let her keep the fucking baby, just to show that I was a decent guy. And what thanks do I get?" He eyed Sade with disgust. "She wants to leave the life of luxury. Go live a simple life with her pussy son. Using *my* money that she *saved up.*" He barked a single laugh. "She saved up *my* money, go figure. To give her pussy son a *real* life. I can still hear her fucking whiny voice. See that's what happens when you give to people." He paced before his desk. "They take and take and take."

He spun on Sade and aimed his finger at him. "I made her a success, I gave her everything she needed to become a top—"

Sade dove over the desk, hoping to kill him before he was stopped. He sank his teeth onto his face and bit hard with a roar. When they pulled him off, he spit out the chunk of flesh, embracing the electricity shooting through his body until it all went dark.

****

Mercy finally found the source of ringing and discovered it wasn't a phone but an alarm going off upstairs in the bedroom. She turned it off. 5 a.m. Looking around, she felt creeped out now. Who set it? She examined the clock and saw it was set to repeat. Had Sade done that?

Exhaustion hit her and she stumbled her way downstairs to the little boy's bedroom and laid in the bed. She wasn't sure how long it was before sleep claimed her. Somewhere around the point where she was imagining herself as Goldilocks, falling asleep in the baby bear's bed while the bears were away, and hoping they didn't come back home while she was sleeping.

****

Sade became conscious long enough to have water blasted in his face. It found its way into his lungs and he coughed and gagged on air and water for endless seconds before it stopped. "Your friend Bo is here with us," the voice said. He recognized Mr. Buckles.

"He's not as strong as you are, I'm afraid. We're going with hot and cold compresses for him. Very effective."

Bo's screams ripped the air and Sade threw his weight in the direction of the voice, but whatever he was tied to didn't allow him one inch. Sade blinked and realized his eyes were swollen shut except for a sliver of light. He tried to remember what happened. How long he'd been there. Fists punching his face flashed in his mind. Not an unfamiliar memory though with his line of work. "You're a million miles… away motherfucker," Sade coughed and wheezed, his body numbed out for the most part. "From getting shit from me."

"Who the fuck turned off the lights?" Mr. Buckles muttered.

Silence reigned and Sade prayed that Bo would die quickly. He jerked right at hearing the faintest sound of a weapon with a silencer.

"Excuse me," Buckles muttered with a lethal tone. "Don't go anywhere."

Sade waited in the timeless darkness then froze when red crosshairs in the shape of a crucifix slowly crawled over his leg and stopped at his crotch. His heart hammered with *holy shit*. He jerked his head up and made out a large shadow before him.

"Johnathon." The silky voice signaled an unfettered insanity but it wasn't physical fear that gripped Sade, it was something else. Regret maybe. He'd finally gotten his old wish, to be under the crosshairs of KK, only he'd given up on ever getting the execution and made other plans. "I'm going to untie you and your friend Bo, and we'll be leaving."

A moment of confusion hit him. Did he want to execute them at another location? It didn't matter. Just so he took care of Mercy. "I.. I hid her."

"I know what you've done, son," his tone was easy while loaded with unpredictability. "I know all about you. More than you probably know about yourself," he said so very casually. "We'll chat over coffee later. I need to go get your pal right now." Sade groaned when his arms were released from behind him. Then his legs were cut free.

Was he making a joke? "Bo…" Sade stumbled along, barely able to walk as KK led him. "…they hurt him."

"That they did," he muttered, again his tone was deceptively cool. It could mean he didn't give a shit and it could mean the opposite. "No more talking. Can you walk out of here?"

"I can," he whispered, staggering, barely able to feel his legs.

"Stay at my back and keep moving."

Sade strained to see through his half good eye and glimpsed scattered dead bodies as they made their way out the back and into a waiting vehicle with Bo dangling from the man's shoulder. After he dumped him in the backseat, he went around the car. "Get in and buckle up," he said before sinking into the driver's seat.

Yes fucking sir. Sade still didn't know what this meant but he wasn't about to argue and the second his ass hit the seat, KK punched the accelerator.

"Mercy is..."

"I know where she is."

Sade pushed through the pain in his body and turned his head to finally get a look at the infamous KK. And wow. Just a fit, middle aged man. Could have been a fucking Fed-Ex driver for all anybody knew.

Half smiling, KK angled serene blue eyes at him. "Not what you expected, I see." He checked all his mirrors before giving a tired sounding sigh and mumbling, "I know you have questions son, and I'll try and answer a few for you." He shot Sade a look. "How's that?"

Sade could hardly believe his ears. Who was this dude?

"I'll take that stunned silence as a yes. Here's the rundown. I was in the Navy all my life. I joined because I wanted to be a hero. Lost a sister to prostitution when I was twelve. She was murdered. Not by your father, no, but same kind of shit. I became a Seal eventually and witnessed some pretty fucked up things. I found Mercy in one of the flesh trade houses during a raid. She was ten. I took her out that night, against orders." He gave a light chuckle. "Hard to put a child back down when she's clinging to your neck for dear life screaming, *'Don't leave me! Don't leave me!'*"

"I put her in another place that I thought was safe, and took my demotion. A few months later, when I tried to arrange to get her, I wasn't allowed. So I went AWOL. Disappeared long enough to change my identity and then I came back for her. Turned out the place I'd put her wasn't as safe as I thought, and she'd been sold again. Not a problem. I found her and killed every motherfucker remotely attached to her pain.

"Then I retired. Raised her off the grid. Made sure—"

"You trained her."

He looked at him a few seconds. "You felt some of that?" He let out a low laugh. "Wanted to make sure she could handle anything that might come her way."

"She can, just about. But how do you know where she is?"

"I always know where she is." His silky confidence soothed him, even if it wasn't intended to. "I think you need to check our pal."

Terror gripped Sade as he spun and looked at Bo. He reached and searched his wrist for a pulse knowing in his gut there wouldn't be one. At finding the faint thumping with his finger, Sade put a hand over his eyes. "Little shit is fucking alive," he gasped. The relief of it made Sade sag into the seat. "He's a tough kid."

"Just like you."

Sade still couldn't discern his tone, it could be good or bad coming from a cold blooded killer. He had so many things he wanted to ask him. Even half dead, Sade couldn't shake the feeling of awe. He was sitting in the car with his hero. That turned out to be his girlfriend's dad. Unreal.

"Go ahead and ask," he said. "The air is crackling with your curiosity."

Sade didn't need to be told twice and he wasn't about to waste the chance. "Why did you fake your death?"

"Many reasons."

His tone said that was all he was getting on that for now. Sade thought for a moment, thinking of the things he really *needed* to know versus *wanted* to know. "Did you know Mercy was going to find me?"

He gave a boisterous laugh and shook his head a little. "My sweet Mercy. Always the optimist, she was. Her finding that envelope was supposed to go much different. She was supposed to bring that to authorities, which would've got you put in prison, and out of my way to finish a job. Not once did I ever consider she'd make the wrong assumptions."

"What… was I going to prison for?"

"That hit and run. You killed me."

Holy shit.

"Only our little Miss Mercy…" he shook his head. "She thought you were my next mercenary assignment. And while you were…"

"I was?"

"Mercenary in your favor. I was getting you out of the way, son, to deal with the devil, your father, no offense." His tone lowered to a note Sade guessed belonged to the man who branded testicles and cut dicks off for a living. "You're nothing like him. You take after your mother."

"My mother," Sade's heart hammered now. "You knew her?"

He didn't answer immediately. "I did, yes."

"How?"

"I know everybody remotely connected to you."

This news baffled him. "Why?"

"Because you were her son and she was my friend," he eyed him, his gaze hard like his words. "I gave a shit about her, that's why. I have a special set of bullets for your father. His death isn't going to be quick. Or clean. Or merciful." He capped that with a happy little smile.

Sade didn't care one bit about how his father would die. "So you know how she died?" Sade had heard several mixed stories.

Kane glanced at him. "What did you hear?"

Sade's body trembled as he shrugged and looked out the window. "That it was an accident." The words gushed out, hoarse.

Kane suddenly gripped his shoulder tight. "It wasn't your fault son. And I can assure you that the last thing she'd want you to fucking do is hate the little boy she loved."

"What else did you know about her?" Sade gasped, wanting more memories than he had. He had so few good ones.

"I know she was an amazing woman. I was going to help her get out and I vowed to watch over you."

He struggled to breathe. "You did?"

"I goddamn did," he muttered with a little laugh. "They fucked with you, they died, it was so very simple. Whether they caught on to that or not didn't matter. I was wiping the slate clean for you son. That's all she ever wanted. Those were her words to me, '*I just want him to have a chance.*' And so I made that happen." He turned with a happy smile and nodded back at the road. "I fucking made that happen, because I'm a doer Johnathon, I'm not a fucking *thinker*, wisher, dancer, or whiner. I'm a fucking *doer*. Can't expect God to do it all now, can we? The man's got plenty to do already, I'm just doing my part and cleaning up my side of the room."

Fucking wow. "Why didn't you tell me?"

"I hoped you'd see it. I hoped you'd figure it out but I couldn't take a chance of you figuring out too many things. And now this." He hit the steering wheel. "We were this fucking close."

Sade collapsed into the door, his body numb now, except for that ache in his chest. He wanted to cut it open and stab his heart over and over until it quit beating on and on and on.

"Listen," Kane said after a while. "I'm going to drop you and Bo off and leave, I can't have Mercy knowing I'm alive. Not until I'm done with Satan. So I need you to not tell her. I need you to wait for me there and not move. If something happens to me, you'll be notified. Can you handle that?"

Damn. "I can, yes. Glad to know you're not killing us."

"Why would I rescue you to kill you?"

Sade shrugged. "Thought you were taking us some place special maybe."

"I had plans, but not these exact ones. Don't you worry, I have plenty of backup games to choose from. It isn't over yet son. No looking back now, do or die, all or nothing. You can be sure of one thing. My life is for Mercy, your mother, and you. That hasn't changed and it never will."

Sade looked at him, baffled by that as an impossible hope surged through him. "Are you... my real father?"

He angled a look at him then fixed a hard gaze on the road. "I won't lie. Many times I wished I was."

Sade's head fell back on the seat. It didn't really matter. It wasn't a father he missed anyway. "She's going to be so happy you're alive. She really loves you."

"Yeah, almost as much as she loves you," he said, sounding offended.

Sade's heart heated and went crazy with those unbelievable words. "I can't… get why," he whispered.

"Me either." His insulted tone was soft and probably the closest thing to verbal kindness he'd get from the man. Which was plenty for Sade.

"But with Mercy," he said. "We can't make promises on life. She mourned my death once and I'd rather leave it that way until this is over. I had become worth too much money and was wanted alive by that fucker Abraham. Me being alive became unsafe for Mercy."

Abraham. Name sounded familiar. "Who is that?"

"The brother of the owner running the largest flesh trade in the world." He shrugged. "He's probably more pissed I soiled his carpet than about me cutting his twin's dick off. Or maybe he's all bitchy because he ate the nasty fucking cock unknowingly for dinner, who knows. It's another reason I'm working from graveside. Some things are easier done when you're dead."

Sade couldn't stop his grin. He really liked this dude. His woman's father of all fucking things. A wave of shock rocked his body at realizing he was about to see Mercy again. Fuck, he had really believed he wasn't going to see her again. That was nearly a given with his karma track record.

"I trust you with her," Kane said. But it carried a clear warning with it.

"Dying for her is as easy as breathing."

"Yeah well don't be a fucking hero, she needs you alive, not dead. We clear? No more lone wolf stunts for you."

The anger in his tone sent a weird warmth through Sade. "We're very clear, sir."

"Good. And same for Bo. And just so you know, he's your half-brother."

"What?" he whispered.

"He's a son of your biological father from his younger days, when he allowed his women to get pregnant. His intention was…" Kane stopped and shook his head a little. "Never mind what his fucking intentions were, they were not nice."

"Does he know?" Sade tossed his head toward Bo.

"Not sure, but I doubt it. Maybe it was mentioned in speculation and he chose to believe the best."

Pain stabbed Sade in his gut at wondering if that's why Bo tried so hard with him. It all made Sade feel like such a fucking dick. A useless human being.

"Don't beat yourself up, you had no idea."

"Yeah well even if he wasn't, I could've had more…"

"Empathy? Compassion? Look, we can all stand some of that bullshit, but in your world those things aren't flashed around. You do what you have to and guard the good stuff, or it gets ripped out of your chest along with your soul. So don't go feeling too guilty. You were dealt a fucking lousy life and you managed your monsters fairly well I think."

Managed his monsters. That's exactly what he had done. "I'm sick of managing monsters, corralling them, trying to appease them."

"That's about to get a whole lot easier."

"What about inside? Dead twenty times over, the bastard will still haunt my body. All my dancing and fighting and trying and I'm still just a prisoner and all visitors are at risk of getting the same fucked up disease I have."

"Yeah well, if it can break it can be fixed," he said, undeterred.

Sade didn't even get how that was remotely possible, but he tolerated the words in that miserable second. He needed something to get through and he was desperate enough to grab any line, just so it kept him hanging on. But there was one thing he was not willing to do, and that was, contaminate Mercy with his shit. His original idea of using her goodness to serve his addictions suddenly burned a path of disgusting shame through him. He needed to protect her from them. Protect her from him. Not invite her in for a taste of something that could lead to hurting her fucking beautiful heart.

Chapter Twenty

Mercy paced with her thumbnail in her mouth. Day two. He said he'd be back and he wasn't. Every possible scenario said he had time to get there, unless he had trouble. She was at the scenario of his body floating in the river. She couldn't wait, she would die, what if he needed her? So what if she would die, how could she fucking live without him *and* her father?

She couldn't. She didn't want to.

Mercy grabbed the keys and her purse and flew to the door and opened it. Like an impossible dream, Sade stood there. She would think he were a ghost except he was so beat up and supported a sagging, half-dead looking Bo.

"Oh my God!" she gasped, covering her mouth. "I was coming! I couldn't wait! I don't care what you say anymore, goddammit!" She ran forward and got under his arm to help him in.

They hobbled to the couch and laid a trembling Bo on it. "What's wrong with him?" she whispered.

"Electrocution I think."

"Oh my God," she turned to him now and looked him over. "You need to lay down," she gasped, leading him to the small bedroom. He didn't argue as she helped him to it. He sat on the bed and pulled her into his lap, hugging her tightly, his face buried in her neck.

"I was about to leave," she choked. "I was coming to find you."

"You promised," he whispered.

"I don't give a shit what I promised, I was coming!" she cried. "I won't be left again, do you hear me? Don't you ever ask that again! I'd rather die with you than die apart from you," she wailed, letting it all out now. "I was so scared to lose you. Scared you would die without me with you! Oh my God, how did you even get here?"

He groaned and laid down, taking her with him. "Hitched a ride. Walked a ways." Slowly he covered her with his leg and pulled her close against his chest. "Mercy," he whispered, already half out of it. "I missed you so bad. Feels like… years since I touched you," he mumbled, barely conscious now.

"Shhh," she whispered, looking for a place to stroke that wasn't beat up. She settled for his chest. "I'm here, I'm not moving ever again." She snuggled her cheek against his chest. "I love you," she whispered softly.

****

Sade woke up to smell of bacon, first. He pried his eyes open and pain shot down his face then rippled throughout his body, letting him know the damage. Turning his head slightly brought a wave of agony that sent him back into a fetal curl inside, where he hid in the darkness till the storm blew over.

But the storm lasted a while with Mercy appearing randomly in the dark waves, forcing him to drink warmth. That's all he knew. He remembered Bo every time he surfaced and wanted to ask but wasn't able.

The smell of something sweet woke him again, along with pain in his groin. Bits of memory came, the most important one being Mercy. She was with him. Taking care of him. And Bo. But where were they? He opened his eyes and released a breath at discovering little pain. She was no doubt medicating him. He looked left and narrowed his gaze at the oddly familiar child's room. Where the hell was he?

It hit him all at once. His room. He closed his eyes as a mixture of dense pain radiated inside him. He was in his childhood bed. In his childhood home.

The door opened and his heart hammered at seeing Mercy slip in with something in her arms. Clothes? He became aware that he was naked at that point. Fuck, it was his bladder that was killing him. He waited for her to look his way, his chest hot with desperate hunger just to feel her in any way. She seemed to sense him staring and jerked her gaze to him. Sade's heart tried to burst at the immediate tears that sprung to her pretty green eyes. She hurried over and laid her head on his chest, exactly where he wanted it.

She stayed that way, both of them silent as he stroked her head and body as far as he could reach. She finally looked up and kissed him all over his face, her tears still streaming with light whimpers now. Her fingers caressed with a tenderness and he'd never felt anything more heavenly. Ever.

He held her face then, staring into her eyes before pulling her to his lips for a soft, lingering kiss. He only stopped because of his pain. "I need the bathroom."

"I'll get something," she said.

He held her arm and she turned. "Help me to the bathroom."

"Are you sure?" She got off the bed and helped him sit. "Of course you're sure."

"How's Bo doing?" he asked, pressing his weight on his feet to see how much strength he had.

"He's so much better!" she whispered. "He's not walking around but he's eating on his own now."

"How long have we been here?"

"You got here two days ago. I had to go into town and buy supplies, there was nothing here to accommodate two broken bodies.

I used cash and talked to nobody," she assured at seeing his concern. "Nobody knows about this place you said?"

He shook his head but the look on her face said she thought otherwise. "Nobody," he added emphatically.

"Okay," she whispered, but the skepticism was there. Sade didn't feel like explaining anything yet, his bladder demanded his full attention.

"I should have run a catheter for you, I'm sorry," she whispered at seeing him grimace. "You'll have to go naked, your clothes are clean but aren't on you."

Sade would have smiled at the obvious but he needed the fucking bathroom too bad. He finally made it and braced a hand on the wall, his entire body trembling from the exhaustion of the short trip. Wow. He was fucked up.

"I'm going to draw you a hot bath, that will help speed up your healing. I've got the ingredients for it but it's upstairs."

Upstairs? Was like the fucking moon to his body.

"Consider it physical therapy getting there. I'll help."

He sighed and allowed her to lead him. He liked how she read him like a book a lot of times, but by the time they made it to the top of the stairs, he didn't like her at all. "Jesus Christ woman. Is this how you came by your name?" he gasped.

"I'm so sorry," she whined, still insisting he move along. "Don't stop now, you're almost there. You got this Rocky!"

"If I fall down the stairs, I'm taking you with me," he warned, out of breath.

"I'll let you catch your wind, then it's on to the tub."

"Mount Everest for the win," he gasped. "Wow, I'm fucking sweating."

"Stop being a whiny baby," she laughed, getting under his arm for the rest of the way.

Sade didn't argue, he needed a crutch. He sat on the edge of the tub once in the bathroom, ready to pass out.

"You look like shit," she cried.

He angled his head and found her staring at him with furrowed brows, hands on her hips while the water ran. He remembered her dad and let his eyes roll closed. He wanted so bad to tell her. It was like he had the power to resurrect her dad from the grave and wasn't allowed to use it.

"You don't really look that bad," she soothed, coming to stand between his legs.

He latched onto her small body and pressed his face into her stomach, his hands stroking her back. He let out a deep moan of satisfaction and need.

"You missed me?" she whispered, stroking his head all over.

He merely slid his face, mouth, and forehead against her in answer.

"I'll take that as a yes." Her palms roamed his shoulders and back, making him shudder. "Let's get you in the tub," she whispered.

Again, he didn't argue. He was ready to be stronger. This pussy shit was for the fucking birds. He was too vulnerable with no strength while needing to protect her and Bo.

He made his way into the hot water and groaned.

"Feels good I hope," she said, pouring capfuls of some kind of oil into the water. "This stuff is supposed to be good for injuries, a natural analgesic. Smells awful but they say it works."

"Eucalyptus," he muttered, taking a deep breath of it. "I love it."

"Definitely a love-hate aroma." She mixed it into the water and then gave him a wash cloth. "In case you want a little privacy."

He eyed her, wondering. "Do you?"

"No," she assured, "I just… I'm giving you the option that's all. Oh," she said, brows raising. "I've got a surprise. I'll go get it and check on Bo while I'm at it."

He closed his eyes and laid his head back, putting the washcloth over his face.

"K, be right back," she said. "Are you thirsty?"

He shook his head, too tired to talk. Not trusting himself to talk really. She was acting... skittish with him. Hiding something it felt like.

She returned with a tray and set it down. "I went to the library in the town, don't worry, I paid cash, and got...this." She spun with two books thrust toward him. "Ta-dahhh. An erotic horror and mushy romance!" She held up one. "Please Don't Leave Me, by Anita Lover, aaaand," she held up the other, "The Pain Seekers by Lady Dom."

He patted the edge of the tub and she came and sat, then hopped back up with an *oh*. She set the books on the tub then went to the tray and returned with a bowl and spoon. "Soup is good food, especially mine."

Sade stared at her, hungry for everything but soup. He was also needing reassurance on a few things. "Can I see you?"

She regarded him with wonder.

"All of you. I'm not hungry. For food."

She set the soup down and gave all the signals that made his stomach knot.

"It's okay," he said, putting the rag back over his face.

"No, I don't mind, I just don't want…"

He pulled the washcloth off to see her expression. Confused. Unsure. Awkward. Afraid. His stomach burned as he slid the washcloth back in place. She was having second thoughts. Not a surprise. He didn't fucking blame her. She had time to get her head straight, no doubt, maybe realized she'd bitten off a little more than she could chew with her charity project.

"I'd like to just be alone please," he mumbled behind the washcloth.

She was silent before finally managing a casual, "Are you sure?"

So she wouldn't fight for it. "Very. Thank you. Maybe later on the reading."

"Okay."

His stomach knotted at the pain in her voice. She was still struggling with those empathy feelings. Damned things were hard to shake for an angel. He'd have to help a little.

"Take care of Bo," he said.

"I am," she said back, sounding defensive.

"I didn't mean to imply you weren't," he mumbled. "I mean don't worry about me, I'm fine."

"Well… I'm sorry but I am worrying about you," she said at the door. "You'll have to deal with that."

So why was she leaving? Sade sighed when the door shut. She'd make this harder than it needed to be. Maybe she was just shaken up from everything. Maybe he needed to give her a fucking break, a chance to prove she wasn't sorry for… being with him.

Chapter Twenty One

Sade made his way downstairs after his bath and found Mercy on the floor kneeling on Bo's back. "Just be still, please," she whispered.

A stab of possessive fury hardened his cock of all things. Stupid fucking body. Only his cock would get hard when angry. Would anger ever equal just fucking anger for him? Would a woman's soft body equal needing to fuck? Ever? Likely not.

Sade clotheslined the sadomasochistic bullshit with a fury, and focused on more important things. "Bo man, you okay my brother?"

Bo groaned and turned over on his side and Mercy flew off of him like she'd been caught doing something wrong. Sade didn't like the guilty reaction.

"I'll see about supper," she said.

Sade eyed her as she scurried off, his gaze unable to not grab hold of her ass. His body was going to be a motherfucker all the way, he realized.

"Sade, we made it!" Bo sat up and laughed, reaching up to take Sade's hand.

He pulled Bo up and embraced him for a brief hug. "We did. Barely, but we did. You okay, my brother?" he asked again, quieter.

Bo lowered his head and nodded. "I'm gonna make it man," he said lightly, giving him a sheepish look and happy little smile.

Sade pulled him into another embrace, needing to love on the kid. He ruffled his hair and smacked his neck lightly. "Thank you man. I owe you." He held his fist up to Bo and they tapped knuckles.

"No thanks needed. Told you I was your bro, didn't I?"

"You did," Sade grinned and pushed Bo playfully off of him. "Mercy taking care of you?"

"Ah yeah," he nodded, moving back to the couch.

Sade eyed his slow decent. "You still hurting?"

"Little bit," he braced one hand on the top of the couch. "Back hurts a good bit."

"Where at?" Sade made his way over and sat next to him. "Show me."

Bo touched the lower right side of his back.

"Where else are you hurting?"

He shook his head. "That's about it."

Sade pressed a few spots on his front abdomen and determined it might be his kidney. "You remember what happened?"

He nodded, not looking at him.

"Okay, man." Sade grabbed his head and pulled it to his shoulder. "You're a tough little dude, you know that?" Sade lightly pushed him away again.

Bo smiled but the trauma of what they'd done to him was all over his face. "I don't want to go through that again," he said, his eyes wide.

"No shit," Sade said. "Maybe we should take up safer hobbies. Like fishing."

It was a joke but Bo's face lit up with amazement at the idea. "I never fished before."

"Never fished before?" Mercy said as she came in and set a tray of food on the coffee table. "We'll need to fix that, won't we? I happen to be an excellent fisherwoman." She straightened and put her hands on her hips. "Go on," she pointed at the tray. "Eat your sandwiches and soup. Get your strength."

Sade looked at her only to have her avert her gaze almost immediately before heading back to the kitchen. He looked at Bo now and realized he was acting weird all of a sudden. What the fuck happened between them?

Sade's anger boiled instantly and he headed to the kitchen.

Mercy shut the pantry door. "Oh shit!" she gasped finding Sade there, waiting.

"What's up?" he asked.

She put a can of something on the counter, eyeing him with wonder. "What... do you mean?"

"Why are you acting weird with Bo? Why is Bo acting weird when you come into the room?"

Her face tightened in a grimace. "I had to help him to the bathroom," she whispered. "It's been kind of awkward since."

That possessive fury shot through the roof but Sade held it at bay. "I imagine so," he said, watching her.

She gave wide eyes and pressed lips while putting her hands in her back pockets. "Yeah, really feel bad for him but somebody had to do it."

Sade had to know. "How exactly did you help him?"

"With a jar," she whispered. "I didn't even look, it was under the covers." She shook her head, "I didn't touch him. His... you know."

His stomach loosened a bit. She'd answered the question that he really hadn't wanted to ask but needed to know. He suddenly missed her so fiercely. Missed her smell, the feel of her body on his. Judging by the way she suddenly lowered her gaze, it showed in his eyes. But her reaction served to steal his oxygen.

He lowered his head, the pain in his chest making him clench his eyes shut.

"Are you hurting?" she asked, sounding genuinely worried.

"Nah."

"You need to go rest now."

Go rest. For some reason the suggestion felt like she was needing to be away from him. Didn't she want to fucking touch him the way he wanted to touch her? Didn't she hurt to hold him the way he wanted to hold her?

Stupid fucking body with its stupid fucking needs that never made a lick of fucking sense. He'd never hated himself more than he did in that stupid fucking second.

He walked off and went to the bedroom and shut the door. Falling asleep turned out to be easier than he imagined but he ended up having an old nightmare. The one with his mother. Where he'd seen that look. The one she gave him just before his father had shut the door and beat her. The look was desperate. Terrified. For herself, for Sade. It said please don't interfere. *I can take him hurting me but not you.* Sade would cover his ears but he couldn't block out the endless sounds of his fist hitting her. The sounds of her falling and his mind drawing the pictures on its own of what was happening. Her grunting and gasping. The way she didn't scream or cry out. Refusing to ask for help or fight back. Just taking the beating like a good mother should. Taking the pain, taking the punishment so that he wouldn't have to. All for him. All for Sade. Anything and everything for Sade. Without a regret.

But Sade regretted. He regretted everything. He regretted being her son, he regretted being alive. He regretted being the one that made her want to live. He had just wanted to take the pain for her. He'd wanted to take the beatings for her. He could do it. He tried to make his father beat him instead, but he'd always make her take it. No matter what, it would end up her fault. She was the reason Sade was born, she was the reason he was a little pussy, she was the reason he needed mommy all the time.

Sade jerked up in bed and found Mercy there, sitting next to it. "Hey," she hurried to his side and pulled his head to her chest.

He gripped her tight and gasped for air then remembered the truth. The pain enraged him and he pushed her off and laid down with his back to her.

"Okay, that is e-nough, mister," she gasped. "Turn over and let's get this over with."

Okay, fine. He turned over. "Get what over with? There is no need to get anything over with, it's already over."

She sat there with her mouth open. "What are you talking about? Why are you acting like this?" she said exasperated.

"You're the one that's different baby. And that's okay. I get it. You had a few days to catch your head, think things over. Realize your little charity project gone wrong is a little too much for you to handle."

She shook her head, "No! You're wrong."

"I can see it Mercy, don't fucking lie and make it worse."

"See what? Me not knowing how to act around you because I'm scared?"

He sat up and stared at her. "Scared of what?"

"Of you! Okay?"

"No, not okay. Explain yourself."

"What is this place, Sade?"

"What?"

She spread her arms out. "Does anybody know about this place?"

"I already told you that."

"Then how is it lived in?"

"It's not," he said.

"Who is all this stuff for?"

"Me," he answered.

"And the stuff upstairs?"

He cocked his jaw and squinted his eyes, trying to figure out what she was assuming. "A woman, why?"

"Well… what woman!"

"Why does it matter?"

"It matters!"

Sade wasn't sure why he needed to do it but he just did. "A girlfriend."

Her brows popped up. "A girlfriend? I thought you said nobody knew about this place?"

"Nobody does but me and her."

"And where is she?"

Sade looked down. "She's not here."

"No shit asshole!"

Desire slammed Sade at feeling her fury. "Why? Do you want to meet her? She's very beautiful, I think you'd like her."

Sade watched as a kaleidoscope of emotions hit her face one after another. She spun around but he'd seen it before she had. Pain.

Of course his body would give him exactly what he didn't expect and especially what he didn't want. The exact same thing. "Am I to understand that me having another woman bothers you, Mercy?"

"Fuck you," she whispered.

"Look at me, Mercy. Say that to me."

She spun around and stormed to him, putting her finger in his face. "Fuck. You," she grit. "And fuck whatever fucking whore you have in this house!"

Sade grabbed her and threw her on the bed, covering her body.

"Get off of me or I'll hurt you," she gasped.

"Hurt me," he breathed back. "I don't think you could do more damage than you have."

Tears spilled from her eyes and her brows crimped. "I haven't done shit to you," she choked. "I've only tried to help you."

"Help me?" he growled. "I don't want your fucking help or your fucking pity."

"What do you want from me? I'll give it, whatever you want, whatever you need," she whispered, heatedly. "Why are you trying to hurt me?"

He stared down at her, not sure how to answer that.

"Having another girlfriend? Here?" Her face crimped harder. "I will kill her, I swear to God."

All the anger suddenly left Sade and he rolled off and sat at the edge of the bed. "You don't have to," he said, emptiness overwhelming him. "I already killed her." He shoved her soft touch off of his shoulder. "Don't fucking touch me."

"Sade, talk to me. Help me understand."

He stood and paced, the anger and fury suddenly boiling over at the stupid *understand* word. There was no point in understanding, what the fuck did understand do? "It's simple, doc. The other woman is my fucking mother and I already killed her. All this stuff?" He started ripping the hero posters off the wall and knocking things over. "This is all my shit, all the shit I was supposed to have. This house is our dream house, that room is my mother's bedroom. Everything here is a reality that never happened, I built good memories see? These are our fucking memories that we planned to have but never did! The memories we stayed up at night talking about, planning, that bed you're sitting in," he pointed, "is my fucking casket. Pretty neat casket, right? This home is my grave, I was coming here to die in peace if you must fucking know. I wasn't stupid, I wasn't ever going to be free of my father so this is where I chose to die, this is my fucking burial ground, my *fate* my *deserving fate* because she was trying…" his voice broke on him, "to buy her freedom… to give me a better life. That bastard beat her…" he shook his head at her. "I saw it. Then he shut the door so I couldn't see, I could only hear. She wouldn't cry, she wouldn't want me to hear, she told me that, Mercy, she told me she hated when he did that in front of me because…" Sade fought to breathe, gasping for air. "…It made her feel…like a bad mother."

His strength left him and he collapsed to his knees, crying. "And… I never saw her again, I never fucking saw her again, not even in a casket. They buried my mom and I never got to say goodbye and then…" he whispered hoarsely, "then you came along, you fucking came along. I wasn't supposed to meet you Mercy. I wasn't supposed to ever… want that love again. But I do," he said heatedly, "I fucking do want it, I'm sorry."

Chapter Twenty Two

Sade jolted with Mercy's embrace from behind. "Sade!" she cried. "You have it! You have my love, I do love you, look at me." She got in front of him and held his face. "I'm scared of you because I'll die if I lose you. I'm scared I'll never be enough, or what you need. I'm scared you'll send me away," she sobbed, hitting him in the chest. "I can't lose you! I love you! I just want to be good enough for you!"

Sade pulled her into his arms at hearing those words. "Mercy," he gasped. "Say it again."

"I love you," she cried holding him tight. "I love you so much. I never want to be apart from you."

"I'm too fucking broken for you Mercy."

She shook her head and cried, "No! Don't say that! I can fix it! We can fix it, and if we can't," she gasped, "we can be broken together, just please let me stay with you and love you no matter what! I don't care if you never have sex with me or if you have weird needs, I love you and I'll help you, that's all I want. Broken or fixed, my heart is yours!"

Sade kissed her, latching his fingers in her hair, the fire from her words overcoming him. He pushed her onto the floor and her passion erupted with clawing and biting. "Don't stop!" he gasped in her mouth, fighting with her clothes without interrupting her perfectly vicious kiss—he never wanted it to stop or end.

"Sade! I need you." Her nails clawed his face then neck, raking down his back and shooting fire into every part of his body, except that one she no doubt wanted it in.

His body didn't seem to care about his limp dick as he continued getting to the source of his need, her nakedness. There was something about it that fed a dark hidden longing in him. Her softness, her warmth, her goodness. It all seemed forbidden to who he was. She was so good and sweet and beautiful, she was everything he should never have and didn't deserve. But craved. He craved her anyway, needed to touch her, explore her, know her so very intimately.

When they were finally naked he meshed her body tight to his with a groan of ecstasy. The impossible connection created havoc in his body, sending his hands to devour every curve and shape, memorizing texture at every crevice and angle. He was so wide open to her, bare in every way as he consumed her smell, the exotic taste of her silky skin. His lips, tongue, and teeth were on a rampage to get it all, get it before it was snatched away. And fuck, her moans and sweet cries, they stole his mind and breath while fueling this strange fire.

She wrapped her legs tight around his waist, and fight instincts instantly hardened his muscles. She gasped and Sade realized his cock had hardened too. Seeming to know his struggle and the balance he was fighting, she raked her nails down his chest, a challenge in the sparkle of her green eyes.

Sade answered with a slow roll of his hips, his cock sliding along her folds. She was wet and so fucking hot on him.

She let out a sexy hiss and dug her nails in his hips. The pain shuddered through him and his sadism reared up, wanting to hurt, wanting him to close his eyes and hide while it had its way.

"Me, Sade," she gasped.

He opened his eyes, falling forward, his hands on either side of her head.

"Look at me," she whispered. "You're mine," she said. "Stay where I can see you."

Fire erupted inside him again and he waited to see what it would do, where it would go. She rocked her hips now, her nails raking his sides.

"You like that?"

Yes he fucking did. He gasped and rolled his hips against her again.

"Yes," she whispered, arching her back while holding his gaze. "Don't you dare stop," she whispered, putting her hands above her head. "Make me, Sade. Take my body. Punish it. Punish me with pleasure," she begged.

He grabbed tight hold of her wrists with one hand, kissing her hard. Her desperate whimpers tickled along his sadism, turning his groans hungry and his cock harder. Then she leaned up for his kiss and her hunger for him, knowing what it meant and how deep it ran through her, sideswiped him.

"Take your time," she whispered, "you got this."

Sade gasped and sucked at her neck, marking her hard with his desperate need to… *be a fucking man for her.* "Fuck, Mercy." He kissed along her jaw, rubbing his face along hers, getting lost in the feel of her skin on his mouth. It derailed his body's usual direction and threw off his fragile momentum he'd gained. "I…" He laid his forehead on her shoulder, breathing.

"Listen to me," she whispered in his ear. "Where am I? Am I right here? Do you feel me here with you?"

"Yes," he nodded, his eyes closed.

"This is where I belong. Are you listening to me baby? Broken or whole, you're all mine. Your body is all over the place?"

He nodded again. "Yes."

"You don't know what to feel, how to control it."

He shook his head, calming, sliding his nose along her neck.

"Do you realize what's happened?"

"I broke my dick," he whispered.

"You're using your heart, baby. Your emotions. Your body isn't used to it, that's all, give it time to catch up. I'm very patient and even more stubborn than you know. Do you know how excited I am to help you with this? We're learning this together. What can't we accomplish? Two hard headed mules like us?"

A warm feeling made him smile and he nudged her face with his nose, kissing his way to her mouth.

"I have plenty of ideas to help you too, help both of us. I have things to learn too."

"Do you?" He laid next to her, head propped on his hand, looking at her. "Like not hiding yourself from me?"

"I'm not hiding," she whined a little.

"You kinda are." He moved her arm off her breast. "If you want me to be open with you, you have to trust me too."

"I do trust you."

He looked at her and she closed her eyes.

"I just have… some memories that are hard to forget."

"Me too," he said, kissing her nose.

She suddenly sat up with an eager breath. "Why don't we try to share our worst memory with each other while we hold hands? Maybe naked even?"

Sade liked the naked part. "How about in the tub." Sade fantasized about sucking her pussy while she sat on the edge of it.

"Ohhhh that's a good idea. Aroma, bath therapy."

"With your orgasm for dessert?"

"And yours?"

He shrugged, moving to kneel before her. "I don't mind letting you try." He did mind her not succeeding though. For her sake.

She looked at his cock and bit her lower lip. "I can bite you maybe," she made a snapping noise with her teeth and it actually got him hard. She quirked a brow at his cock then looked up at him. "I got your number baby. And before you know it, I'm going to call it out and boom. It's on."

He smiled and pulled her to her knees, stroking her hair while she kissed his chest. "I can't wait."

"You are looking at a master in the making. I will command your body with one little look," she said with a sultry boldness.

His heart sped up at those words. Deep down, he longed for that. "I'm rooting for you, angel."

He pulled her to her feet and they got dressed. Peeking out of the room, they hurried upstairs like two kids in a race, trying not to wake Bo on the couch. When they got to the bathroom, they helped undress each other then he pulled her body to his, sliding his hand along her pussy. "I need to bring you," he whispered, dipping his finger in her. The hunger to do something he *could,* hit him like crazy.

"How about I bathe. And make you."

His cock hardened and she smiled under his mouth. "My body always has a good reaction to that idea."

"We'll need to make a note," she whispered.

"Already noted."

She pulled away and got the bath ready, holding her one forearm over her breasts as she went, almost like an old habit. One he needed to help her break.

"You make me want it more when you hide them, angel."

She glanced up and rolled her eyes at seeing where he stared. "Sorry." The sweet word came with her lowered arm but Sade realized she now hid in a hunch.

He climbed into the tub and held his hand for her. She took it and he had her sit on his stomach. "Let me just look at you."

She took in a deep breath and looked up, allowing him. But it was hard for her. He reached and stroked her precious mounds, finding them absolutely perfect. "I love your tits," he said, eyeing her face for her reaction.

She lowered her head and stared at the water while holding his wrists, her grip tense. "Thank you." But it was hard, he could tell. She was making herself. "Is that how you do it?"

She looked at him. "Do what?"

"Re-learn things. You say the right thing even when you don't feel it?"

She bit her lip. "That obvious?"

"Very." He lowered his hands to her waist then and held it. "We were going to share?"

He waited to see how she still felt about that. "Yep," she waved her hands in the water, averting her gaze still.

"I want to know," he whispered.

"What would you like to know?" she asked lightly.

"How you learned to be so brave."

She gave a small smile. "My dad taught me. He was relentless, but it paid off. I learned how to fly again."

"You know how to fly, angel?" She eyed him, blushing while Sade stroked over the nipple she hated. "Tell me, Mercy."

She brought her forearm over it and her smile left. Sade felt the weight of the nightmare she held at bay and his need to destroy it hummed through him. The need to know it, name it, own it, crush it.

Maybe if he went first…

"My worst memory," he began, stroking her thighs. "Was when I just turned four." He stroked her cheek and she held onto his hand as the scared little girl peeked out of her eyes again. "My mother… she was so beautiful," he continued.

"Is that her in the picture?" He nodded and brought her hand to his lips, kissing her fingers. "She was, very much so."

"She would have adored you, Mercy," Sade said, sure of that. "One of the things my mother tried really hard to do was protect what I saw. She was really big about protecting my eyes when it came to her job. She was a drug mule and a paid prostitute by my old man." Sade took a deep breath and Mercy suddenly laid on his chest, holding him. He stroked her head, hoping that sharing this hell would somehow unlock something good for them. Didn't have to be heaven, just an outer garden would do.

"On my birthday she uh. She complained to my father about how the men were touching her in front of me and could he please talk to them. He didn't like her tone, knocked her around as usual. Called her ungrateful and other names. Then…" Sade paused a moment. "Then he said he'd show her a bad example. Two men came a little later and my father made me watch while… they raped my mother. But she screamed and fought and cursed the entire time. I tried to close my eyes and he'd shake my head and yell for me to look. *'Look what happens when your mother talks back to me. Look what she brings!'*

"Then one of the men screamed in pain. My mother had bit him."

Mercy bolted up, staring at him with wide eyes, mouth open.

"And she had him good, she was so angry, she wouldn't let go of his dick no matter how much they beat her. I screamed as loud as I could when my dad picked up a lamp and hit her with it. She fell on the floor and didn't move. I wanted to cover my eyes but I needed to see my mom, I had to watch out for her, so I couldn't stop looking. And my father went out and came back in with something in his hands." Sade's voice shook and he wiped his mouth, fighting to keep control. "You want to bite?" The words broke on a gasp. "I'll teach you to bite. And he… he started pulling her teeth out… with fucking pliers!" Mercy latched back onto him, sobbing and hugging him. Sade held her hard to his body, rocking with her, unable to stop the words now. "She screamed! She screamed and screamed until her voice was gone, so I screamed for her! It was my birthday and I was four, I still had my Superman cape on. And I used my biggest voice and I screamed, I screamed with all my powers for her!

"And he finally left," he gasped. "She crawled to me and there was… so much blood all over her fucking mouth but she covered it with her hand, to hide it. She hid the sight from me, protecting my eyes. 'Shhhh, shhhh,' she fucking said to me," he strained. "'Mommy's okay, mommy's ok.' But she was screaming the words, she wasn't fucking okay," he gasped. "She held me and rocked me while screaming mommy's ok."

Mercy sobbed uncontrollably, strangling his neck and Sade held her just as tight.

"I'm sorry," she cried, her voice hoarse and bitter. "I'm so sorry, you were just a baby! You were just a baby!" she cried. "And your mother was so good! She was so good!"

He gasped and kissed her neck, pressing his face into her warmth, into that piece of heaven he'd somehow ended up with. Just having her with him in that moment ripped him open and his own bitter sob wrenched out of him as he continued to rock her.

After a little while Mercy pushed off of him suddenly. "I'm going to tell you what happened!" she gasped.

Sade shook his head, "you don't have to angel."

She nodded roughly. "I am," she demanded in an angry sob. "I'm not going to let it push me around anymore, I want to tell you and I want you here for me," she grit, holding his hands to her chest. "You said I can confess to you and I need to confess," she strained bitterly, tears pouring.

Sade pulled her to his shoulder, holding her head, stroking it. "Okay angel. Let it out. Let it go, I'm right here, you're safe."

A sob tore from her and she pulled away, looking at him. It was like his own confession brought her to the edge and she wasn't going to back down now. But she had to hurry and jump or she'd never try again. But fuck he was suddenly not sure he could handle her pain. His own was one thing, hers was another.

Chapter Twenty Three

Mercy wiped her eyes with the heels of her hands and sniffled. "I never confessed this yet," she whispered. "I tried. I knew I should for so long and I kept thinking I could just…" she shook her head and her face crimped, making Sade lean forward and kiss her, hold her.

"Shhhhh, angel, I'm here. Right here."

She nodded. "Okay. So… I was nine years old. I'm going to say this fast," she wailed. "I can't go slow, okay?"

"Yes baby, run through it, I'm right here."

"So I was nine." The words gushed loud with the force of her trauma, making Sade nearly panic. "I was at a bad, bad, place. A place with other kids, a lot of them," she whispered, as though not wanting to speak the evil too loud. Sade let her hold his hands and she gripped them so tight, they shook. "There were bad men there. They took me to a room," she whispered, her eyes wide, staring before her.

"Look at me Mercy," Sade whispered. "Don't go back there. Stay with me. Tell me."

Her eyes were huge and filled with terror, Sade was ready to fucking stop her. "There was a dog," she whispered. "They made me… do things with it." Her brows furrowed and silent sobs found their way out as her eyes filled with tears. "They made it do things to me," she whispered hoarsely. "The dog was so scary," she gasped. "I tried not to cry, I tried, and they kept hitting the dog and it bit me!" She flew up out of the water with the screamed words, her eyes clenched shut. Sade stood with her and grabbed hold of her. "It bit me!" she screamed, shaking.

"Mercy!" Sade yelled, shaking her.

She snapped wide terrified eyes to him, sobbing uncontrollably now. "It bit me!" she shrieked, pointing her trembling finger to her chest. "It bit me!"

Sade's fury took him and he spun and slammed his fist into the mirror next to the tub, over and over, shattering it to pieces like his fucking heart. He turned and grabbed Mercy into his arms. "I'm sorry angel. I'm so sorry. Look at me," he put her before him. "Look at me baby," he gasped, shaking her a little so she'd open her eyes.

When she gazed at him, his own tears fell. "We're pretty fucked up, angel. So fucking broken, and shattered." He pulled her tight to him again. "I need you. Broken or not, shattered or not, my heart… is yours."

He held her while she cried it out. Worried about glass in the tub, he helped her out and resumed holding her close, *shhhhing* her. When she seemed done, he wiped his eyes on his shoulder and set her before him. "Hey. You want to hear something funny?" He swiped her tears with his thumbs, and stroked her head. "When I was four, I had this jar that I saved money in. Do you want to know what I was saving for?"

She looked at him and gave a pitiful nod.

"A stairway to heaven. For my mom. Like the song?" He tried to smile but couldn't manage it. "She loved it and I wanted to buy it for her." A suffocating pain hit Sade and he grabbed Mercy to hang on to. "I fucking miss her!" he cried with the deep ache.

"I miss my dad! I miss him so bad too."

Sade nearly gushed the truth to her. *He's alive baby! He's fucking alive!* He wanted *so much* to make something right in her life. But what if he fucking *died* again? He clenched his eyes tight and held it in.

Mercy suddenly pushed out of his embrace and paced. A bone deep fatigue hit Sade and he slowly made his way to the floor and laid on the cool tile.

"Oh my God," she gasped, still pacing. "I feel better!" She eyed him in amazement. "Do you? Do you feel a weight lifted? I feel it, I feel... fucking lighter!"

"So good angel," he mumbled.

"I have an idea," she hurried and held her hand down to him.

He regarded it. "Requires getting up?"

"Yes," she said, serious. "Any time I had an epic break down with my dad, he'd always do this."

Sade couldn't help but smile. "We both had fucking epic shit storms just now." She nodded with a little smile and he reached for her hand and let her pull him to sitting. He made his way up and moaned. "Do we do this naked?" He was ready to streak in a church for her at this point because he did feel better he realized.

"No," she giggled, and sniffled. "Oh! Do we have music?"

"Music? I have my phone," he said. "But I wouldn't want to turn it on. To be safe."

She chewed her lip.

"I have an old record player downstairs with a collection of albums."

Her eyes widened with a smile then got serious. "What about Bo?"

Sade thought about it. "He can go in my bedroom?"

She was all smiles again and nodded. "Yes, let's do this!"

She turned for her clothes and Sade eyed her. "And what are we doing?"

"You'll see! Something to fill!"

Sade got dressed and grinned at her. "Something to fill, huh? Guessing not your pussy."

She grinned and stumbled into her jeans then hugged him while he was pulling up his. "We're like this now," she said, holding up two crossed fingers in his face.

He leaned in and bit them then kissed her when she yanked them out of reach. "Two twisted up people? Yes, we are."

She laughed. "No, we're *tight*."

"You're tight. And I didn't eat your pussy like I fucking wanted."

She bit her lip with a smile. "I promise to still *make* you do that. But this first."

"Okay, this first, then that."

"Deal."

They went downstairs and Sade carried Bo into the bed, despite his protests that he could walk. Sade really didn't want to take the time to walk him. He was too eager to see what his sweet Mercy had in mind. She was about to perform more magic for him. And he'd come to learn that when Mercy performed magic, it wasn't tricks. It was the real thing.

Mercy sat on the floor digging through the albums, mumbling the names while Sade made them coffee. "I don't know half of these," she called. A few seconds later, he heard her gasp, "Ohhhhh my God!" He looked over as she ran to him with an album. "Do you know who this is?"

He looked at it. "The Who. I actually do know that band."

Her eyes were wide. "Do you know what *else*?"

He laughed and shook his head, "Nope." He put his palms on the counter watching her flip it over and read.

"Here it is!" She turned it and pointed. "Reign Over Me!"

"I like that song."

"You do?"

"Okay, tell me what's so fascinating about it."

"When my daddy took me home with him, he said I had to take at least one artistic lesson. And so of course I took *ballet!*"

He smiled at that. "Of course."

"And when I was graduating the dance academy, they had this big froo-froo event where you had to perform, and I performed to this song!"

Sade's heart raced at that. "And now you want to perform it for me?"

Her mouth dropped with her narrowed gaze. "God no!"

"What!?" he said offended. "And why not? I've always wanted a girlfriend who danced ballet for me."

She bit her lower lip and eyed him with a gorgeous fucking smile. "You said girlfriend," she whispered.

He reached and grabbed the front of her t-shirt and pulled her to him. "You like that?"

"Very much," she said, smiling more up at him.

"I used to dance too," he said.

Her eyes widened. "You did? What kind?"

He shrugged. "Kinda like… dirty dancing."

Heat flashed in her eyes with her raised brows. "I'll make a deal with you," she said.

"Mmm, my fucking cock is eager to hear it."

She gasped happily and put her hand on it. "It likes to dance?"

"It likes the idea of you dancing."

"I think we're onto something Mr. Ashcroft."

He laughed at that. "Mr. Ashcroft?"

"Sounds so hot, doesn't it?" She pushed off of him and started twirling her hips and arms above her head in a seductive motion that really got him hard. She eyed him over her shoulder now. "Would Mr. Ashcroft like to see me perform… naked?"

"Fuck yes," he whispered.

"Maybe I could…" she stroked her hands over her ass, "make you…touch yourself while I did?"

Anything with the word *make* seemed to result in a hard on for his body. He nodded eagerly with a heated, "Yes," while devouring the twirl of her tight ass.

She suddenly spun and clapped like a little girl. "I'll need room," she whispered before running off to move furniture.

Sade could never get enough of her night and day, hot and cold, sexy and innocent, and how perfect she managed both. He hurried to help, wishing Bo was upstairs now. He could fucking tie his door shut, forcing him to have to knock to get out. He wanted to see her dance naked so bad. Near naked would be just as good since she was still shy. T-shirt and panties would do it for him, he loved the *fuck* out of her cute, tight ass.

When everything was cleared out of the way, Sade found a bungee cord in the kitchen and attached it to the bedroom doorknob.

"What are you doing!" she whispered, laughter in her voice.

"Making it so you don't have to worry about company."

"Or so that you don't have to worry?"

"Yeah, that too," he angled a look at her with a grin at hearing how she liked that.

"I like that you're possessive," she announced in quiet secrecy.

He turned and pulled her against him, grabbing her ass. "You have no idea. Will you dance in your panties for me? You get to keep your shirt on," he added nicely.

She grinned. "How merciful."

"I learned from the master." His hands were on the front of her pants.

"I haven't danced in years," she whispered shrilly.

"No backing out," he ordered.

She worked her hips and he helped get her pants off. He went and sat on the couch and put an arm over the top, staring at how fucking adorable she looked in her red t-shirt and white brief panties.

She made her way to the record player and began stretching, giving him various angles of her tight ass. Then she put her back to him, spread her legs apart and bent over, palms to the floor. "Ffffuuuuck, yes," he said, staring at the perfect outline of her pussy lips in the white cotton. It screamed for his tongue and finger. He allowed himself to imagine his cock in her that way, holding her hips and sliding slowly in and out. The fantasy had him so fucking hot. Then she looked around her leg with a smile and set off those fireworks in his heart.

Sade didn't allow himself to be entirely derailed. He struggled to work both powers warring in his body for her. He put his hand on his cock, helping himself as she bounced to the left, then right, and popped up, pulling her panties out of her ass. He rocked his hips and groaned while his heart raced with anticipation of what she was about to do for him.

She put on the record and hurried to the center of the room and assumed her position, a ball on the floor with her head tucked in. "I'm very rusty," she warned, her voice muffled. "So don't judge."

"Promise you'll show me the same mercy when it's my turn," he muttered, reminding her of their deal so she didn't back out still.

"Oh my God, I can't believe I'm doing this," he barely heard her whisper.

He couldn't either, what a treasure. The piano music finally started and her legs and lower body slowly ascended into the air until she was doing a handstand, her legs in a perfect split. Fucking. Wow. The strength alone it took to do that was phenomenal, but add her flawless balance and he was blown away.

She was finally on her feet when the *"Only love"* part of the song began. Sade was quickly enraptured with her performance. It was like… her body became a moving picture of the power, need, longing and passion in that song. Her moves slowly increased in speed and vigor, limbs lashing with a perfect fervor. But when the lyrics turned explosive, Sade was at the edge of his seat as every phenomenal jumping split in the air hit *exactly* on that dramatic *"love!"* note.

She landed on one of the jumps and fell with a shriek. Sade flew to her and knelt down where she held her ankle. "Shit shit!" she gasped. "I twisted my damn ankle."

"The carpet baby," he said, breathless, looking at her foot as she hissed in pain while gasping for her wind.

"It hurts, it hurts," she said. "I think it's worse than it looks."

Sade couldn't help but chuckle at those adorable words. "Aww, it's bad baby?"

"It *is!* And don't do like my father and act like it's nothing. I hated how he did that."

He angled a grin at her and stroked her ankle softly. "I think it's swelling."

"Yes!" she exclaimed. "No doubt!"

He lifted her leg and kissed very softly all over the area, eyeing her heaving chest and sweaty face as he did. He just wanted to lick her all over now.

She bit her lip and smiled. "My dad never did that."

He scooped her up and moved her to the couch.

"What about me?" she asked, worried. "What about your dance?"

"I don't know, I guess I could give you half a show."

"That was almost all of it though!"

He leaned in and kissed her softly. "You want to know something?"

"Not about my dancing, no."

He pulled away enough to look her in the eye then sighed and stood. "Guess I won't tell you then."

"I don't want to know if it's not good," she said.

He gasped a laugh, holding a hand on his chest. "Let me just say… why the fuck aren't you dancing professionally?"

She gasped. "You lie!"

"Do I look like the bullshitting type?"

"Really?"

"Mercy, I have never seen anything more amazing. And that's not because you have the finest fucking ass in the fucking world either."

"I do?" she giggled, seeming just as happy over that.

He shook his head at her. "I'm officially disgusted that you don't know that."

She put her hands over her mouth, looking up with her happy sparkly green eyes. "Thank you," she squealed. She flicked her fingers at him with wide eyes. "Your turn. Mr. Dirty Dancing."

Chapter Twenty Four

He sighed and nodded. "I think we should take this upstairs, though. This could end… in a way that requires privacy."

"Oh my God," she whispered, turning into a sweet virgin of sexy innocence. Then she held up her arms. "You'll have to carry me."

Sade scooped her up and she said, "Bo! His door, you better undo it."

He made his way over and fought to undo it while holding her, using the doorjamb to support her.

He finally managed and carried her upstairs, his body humming with that chaotic desire. She opened the master bedroom door for him and he carried her to the large poster bed with the white sheer curtains and laid her in it. He kissed her when she refused to let go of his neck then he finally unlocked her hands.

"What about music," she whispered, biting her lip.

"I brought my phone. I have one saved on it."

"Ohhh, nice. Is this your favorite song?"

"It's one of them, definitely."

She sat up with her legs crossed Indian style and wiggled with an excited grin. "What's it called?" she asked.

"It's called Sail." He smiled while finding the song then handed her the phone. "Just press play when I'm ready."

She bit her lip, eyeing him. "Got it. Sail. Finger on the trigger."

Sade stood next to the bed, shaking his head.

"What?"

"Just can't believe I'm about to do this."

She giggled. "Me either, oh my God, I'm so… hot."

He eyed her and nodded. "That helps."

"It does?" She sat forward and removed her t-shirt and threw it at him then placed her arms behind her on the bed.

Sade returned her naughty smile and eyed her tits. "You didn't need to do that but… I'm very grateful that you did."

She eyed his groin with raised brows. "I see that."

"Yes, you do, don't you? Press play."

She hit the button with an eager sparkle in her eyes and Sade closed his eyes, listening to the music, letting it take him to that place where nothing mattered. At the opening of the song, Sade spun around and vibrated his ass to the dubstep drop, then gyrated his hips in long and short thrusts, matching the pulsing rhythm. He slid his hands up his abs, taking his shirt with him, rocking and twisting his pelvis as he did. He spun and faced her when he removed his shirt, grabbing his cock with both hands, pumping slow then fast, hard then smooth. She squealed, sitting at the edge of the bed now as he worked his jeans down. He dropped to the floor putting them at his ankle then shot back up, his hands back on his cock, dancing his way out of the denim. Desire shot through him at finding Mercy lusting in open abandon, her nipples hard and her back arched, making them stand out. He twirled his hips, making his way toward her. When he reached the bed, he didn't stop, forcing her to lay back as he climbed on. He continued his dance on his knees until he straddled her chest, moving his hips to the music in a fucking motion right above her face.

Mercy got on her elbows and licked at his cock, her fingers stroking over his balls. Sade locked his hands behind his head and hissed, wanting to make her. He closed his eyes when the feelings inside fought to derail each other, focusing on the feel of her mouth and tongue, the rake of her nails on his balls.

Then the song ended and all that remained was the sound of her sweet voice as she sucked him. Sade was willing to *pray* that his cock remained hard for her and it seemed the second he even thought it, his body began turning on him. If Sade wanted it, hurry and run the other fucking way.

"Okay, okay," she sat up between his legs as Sade knelt there with his eyes closed, hating himself. "It's okay." She worked her way to kneeling and hugged his waist. "Look at me," she said before him.

He opened his eyes and stared at her, noting the challenge brewing in her gaze.

"Remember when you asked me to… be a fuck in your sexathon?"

He merely raised his brow and shook his head a little.

"I want to," she said. "I want to be a fuck in your sex thing."

He sat and shook his head. "No fucking way."

"Why?" she asked, sitting next to him.

"Because I can't do that with you."

"What can't you do?"

"I can't have that kind of sex with you."

"What kind is it?"

"It's rough and mean and long and satanic, that's what kind."

"It doesn't have to be."

"I use five women for that Mercy. Because one can't handle it, do you really think I'll fucking use *you* for that?'

"I can take it," she cried.

"You can't fucking take it! I won't do that to you."

"I want you to!" she demanded.

"I don't care what you want. It's not happening."

"What if you tie me up?"

"Oh yeah, and fuck you to death? I don't think so." He was pacing before the bed now, just talking about it had his sadism riled.

"You're hard just talking about it."

"I don't care," he pointed at her. "Not happening."

"Why not! How about I fight you?"

"What?" he squinted at her.

"What if I fight you while I fuck you, huh? If you get too crazy I'll just kick your ass?"

Sade's cock got impossibly hard at that fucking idea. To fuck and fight? At the same time? Could there be anything more arousing to his sadism? No, he was sure there wasn't.

"Ohhhh," she gasped. "You want that."

He held his head and grit his teeth at her. "Yes, I want that, but I will never do it."

"Why not! Come on!" She stormed up to him and slapped his face and he jerked his gaze to her. "Fuck me, fight me, come on!" she yelled, pushing him then punching him.

"Mercy, stop," he yelled.

"I won't stop! I won't stop!" she pushed him again, getting more aggressive.

"I won't fucking be able to stop once I start," he gasped, his hunger slowly taking him for what she begged.

"Then don't stop! Don't stop," she shoved him again. "Do it Sade!" She suddenly let him have it, peppering his front with her Wing-Chun. Sade grabbed her by the shoulders and shook her, then shoved her away.

He paced and gasped, clenching his eyes. "Stop it Mercy, fucking stop! Don't make me!"

But she was hell bent and determined. Fuck. "I'm fucking making you," she yelled, layering his side with rapid kicks.

Sade caught her foot and flipped her, but she landed on her feet, calling him with her hands to bring it.

Sade heaved, staring at her, wiping his mouth. He eyed the blood on his hand. That was it. He felt it. She'd pushed him to that fucking point. He tossed his head left and right, his mouth open with the raw lust roaring through him.

"You want it?" he muttered, walking slowly around her.

"I want it," she whispered. "And I will have it."

He nodded, stroking his cock now. "Bend over the fucking bed."

She shook her head. "You'll have to fight for that one."

That idea made him grin with pure joy. Sade launched for her and she dodged, landing two fucking kicks to his stomach and chest. He slowly straightened, swinging his arms, loosening them. He made another move for her legs and managed to get her on the floor where he wanted her. Grappling ensued and Mercy landed a few face punches before he pinned her arms. Her legs wrapped his waist now and she gasped, winded, staring at him with open mouth.

"What's the matter? Short a hand?" she asked.

Sade leaned in and kissed her, his sadism ruthless as he sucked and bit at her lips. She returned it back the same, driving him crazy. He'd never felt the hunger to taste during sadism like he did in that moment. He grabbed hold of her jaw and turned her face to suck and lick a slow hot path to her ear. Her worried gasps and moans drew his low growl as he sucked the lobe and shell. Sade's breath shuddered with a rumble as he opened his mouth wide and slid it slowly and firmly up and down her neck, scraping with his teeth as he went. He clenched his fingers in her hair and tilted her head back, tasting and sucking the tight silk as his licks and bites grew harder. He growled his way back to her jaw, licking his way to her cheek, then temple. He gripped her head tight in both hands, tasting along her forehead, driving her moans higher.

"Fuck me," she gasped. "Please *fuck me*."

Her harsh demand made him rock hard. "I'm not fucking done tasting you yet." He slid his hands along her arms, continuing his feast on her chest, making his way to her breasts. He gripped the small mounds and squeezed hard enough that she cried out. He opened his mouth and sucked with a hungry groan as much of her tit as he could, extra hungry when it came to his favorite one, perfectly imperfect. He growled and hissed as he bit at her nipple before continuing his tasting along her stomach, his sadism eager to taste her pussy in the worst fucking way. He dug his fingers hard into her waist as he sucked with a vicious need, licking that silky skin and biting her hard muscle.

Mercy raked his scalp with her nails and squirmed beneath him as he made his way between her legs. He held them open wide and pressed them hard to the floor, kissing her pussy with a starving intensity. He meshed his lips against hers, turning his head to get at all of it, licking and lashing at every part. Drunk on his sadism, he lifted his head and gasped, hissing with his eyes closed as he slid his finger inside of her, very slowly. He worked his way to kneeling, staring in a daze at her body writhing on the floor. He placed his hand on her chest, watching her while he moved his finger in her. She pulled her legs back and raised her arms above her head, arching her back and rocking her hips.

He fucked her with his finger, fast then slow. Her mouth remained opened and her brows drawn hard as he rammed his finger hard then pulled out very slowly. He did this until she held his wrist and bucked, dancing with his pace.

Sade grabbed her hips and lifted her off the floor. He opened his knees and placed her pussy on the head of his cock. He locked his gaze to hers, knowing his sadism wouldn't let go now. Knowing he could soul mesh all he wanted and it wouldn't matter. He worked his cock into her, bearing his teeth at how fucking tight she was. He looked down when he was halfway in and gasped, twirling his hips then rolling them slowly while looking at her. He was going deep and he wanted it to be a surprise. He yanked her onto his cock and groaned hard at the shriek she gave him, at the hot vice she clamped him in.

Her cries were edged with whimpers and she latched her legs around him. He closed his eyes tight and stroked her tight ass and hips, still twirling his own. He raked his fingers up her spine then slowly back down before latching onto her thighs again. He grit his teeth, fighting to go slow as he moved her on and off of him. But her fucking gasps and cries… his sadism loved it too much. His nails dug as he moved her faster. His mind kept hearing the song he'd danced to and he rotated his strokes from smooth and deep, to fast and shallow, then deep, hard, and very fucking fast.

Sade fucked her that way until they were both sweating. He lowered her ass and fell forward, grabbing her arms and holding them next to her head as he kissed her mouth like he'd kissed her pussy. He fucked her at the same erratic pace, licking and sucking at her face and neck. He raised up enough to watch her for a while, needing to just see her as he fucked her. Her strength challenged his sadism, calling for more. He'd not really begun. In the back of his mind he watched her. Watched her keeping pace with him. He dared not entertain the idea that she'd make it through unscathed by his sadism.

As time went, Sade slowly became drunk. And then he felt it closing in, that second wind, that point where his sadism wanted complete control, complete freedom. Sade raised up on his haunches and pulled her with him. Still kneeling, he held her hips and showed her what he wanted now. She held onto his neck and wrapped her legs around him, her strength shooting desire through him. He moved her up and down on his cock, letting his head drop back with his eyes closed, breathing through what was slowly taking him. His fingers slowly tightened on her hips and he began moving her faster. He looked down, watching his cock sink in and out, his hips flicking now. His drunk gaze slowly moved up her sweaty body, ending on the column of her neck, fully exposed with the backward tilt of her head as she moaned louder and louder.

Fire licked hot and eager in his groin as he grabbed her shoulders and forced her onto his cock harder, faster. She was finally there, screaming with it. That's where he had to have her. Screaming. He pulled out of her and turned her over on all fours, sliding in from behind with a hiss at how fucking amazing she looked that way. He resumed bucking his hips, his pace relentless, deep, and fast. He pressed her upper body down with both hands, holding her to the floor as he hammered into her, his growls feral and steady. It was the only voice his sadism knew.

She screamed again when his pace and intensity became overwhelming. When his sadism got restless again, he pulled out and laid her on her stomach. She opened for him and raised her ass and he slid inside her. "Fucking yes. "He worked his arm under her chest and held her shoulder while grabbing a handful of her hair. He kept his mouth at her ear as he fucked her slow for the first few minutes. He held her head back and kissed at her face while he ground his cock into her, his body pressed hard into hers.

She began crying out his name, the sound desperate and weak. His hunger spiked and Sade licked along her face, sucking hard, biting even harder.

Her cries were peaked again, delirious sounding. Yes. That. He had to have that, had to have her overcome.

He pulled out again and turned her on her back. Wanting to feel all of her, he meshed their wet bodies and slid his cock into her again, devouring her sharp cry, his hunger somehow more ravenous. He held her neck, his fingers sliding over her wet skin and tight muscle, feeling her cries and moans. Sade fucked her deep and slow, his pelvis never leaving hers for a tight, hard penetration that he worked with his hips.

Mercy showed more signs of wearing down. It soon became less about pleasure and more about enduring. And now his sadism wanted rougher, more.

"I'm not fucking done, Mercy, not even close," he gasped in her mouth.

She gave several whimpers and worked her arms out from under his hold. She grabbed his face and kissed him back with an equal hunger. "Do it. Use me. Fucking do it," she gasped in his mouth before sliding her nails down his back.

Sade let out a roar at the burning trail she carved in his skin. He raised up on his hands and began hammering his cock into her, eagerly taking the challenge. Her tits bounced and she wrapped her legs around him again. She raked her nails along his neck, again tearing skin, driving his fire higher. The pain mixed with his sadism for a fucking dirty bomb of pleasure. His growls came louder as he continued the relentless pounding, fighting to taste her everywhere, biting at her mouth and face, her neck and nipples.

She suddenly leaned forward with a small half scream then collapsed down, her palms on his chest. Her head lolled and her eyes met his, slit with desire and fatigue now. She bared her teeth and opened her mouth, then dug her nails into his chest, raking the flesh away.

Sade growled and devoured her shoulder blade, biting harder. She screamed again and grabbed his neck.

The masochistic act put rocket boosters on his sadism. Sade gave a raspy groan of pleasure, hoping she didn't stop. He slowed his pace as though his sadism knew she was the only thing available to use and wasn't ready to break her. He didn't slow for long though and went back to fast and hard, the jolt in her cries feeding his fire.

She switched hands on his neck and squeezed hard, the act ramping up his speed. She gasped and bared her teeth again before she gave a long strained roar.

"Fuck. Fuck yes!" he seethed. "Do it!" he grit, his body thrashing against her.

She screamed again, her eyes sparking with sheer determination as she used two hands to choke him, digging her nails in. Sade focused on all the power she created. The piercing grip on his neck, the vice on his cock, the way he hit hard bottom with the head of his dick, the fucking sound of him slamming into her pussy as fast as he could to bring those jolting, desperate shrieks. That was it. Her concoction was just what his sadism fucking wanted and it took it, took it all at once, tearing Sade's throat with a roar of suppressed fury. The orgasm came in vicious waves, each shooting his hot seed deep inside her. The fact that he didn't have the sense to pull out as he always would, told him just how mindless he'd become, how far she'd taken him.

He finally fell onto Mercy, both of them breathing like they'd fought for their lives for over an hour rather than fucked. Sade barely shook his head at the bad fucking idea he'd just succumbed to. His first time having sex with his angel… was sadistic. Ruthless and sadistic. No emotion, just cruel and reckless grinding.

"I love you," she gasped in his ear.

Chapter Twenty Five

Sade pulled out and rolled off of her, feeling so fucking… dirty and evil. He stumbled to his feet, not able to look at her.

"Wow," she whispered.

He finally looked at her, afraid of what he'd find. Then he saw it. Blood on the carpet. Rage slowly overtook him and before he realized what was happening, Mercy's screams were a hum in the back of his head as he crushed and broke everything his hands touched. When there was nothing left, he stumbled in the debris, his every breath a hoarse roar.

Mercy stood crying in a corner and Sade fell to his knees. He covered his face, still furious that the pain was no better. "I didn't want to hurt her!" he roared to nobody and anybody. "I didn't want to fucking hurt her, I just wanted to *love her!*" he thundered. Mercy was suddenly holding him and he covered his head.

"Don't shut me out," she cried. "Don't you dare shut me out!"

She began hitting him and shoving him and he collapsed to the floor, surrendering to her. "Mercy," he whispered, pulling her to him. "I don't deserve you, I don't fucking deserve you. I didn't want to hurt you."

"Sade, Sade," she gasped in his face, tapping it with her hand. "Look at me. Look at me."

Sade finally did, even though it was so fucking hard to.

"Don't you see? Don't you see what we just did? How can you not fucking see!" she yelled at him.

"See what baby, I'm so fucking blind, I can't see shit."

"I did it!" she cried. "Don't you see? I did it! I helped you. How many women am I? How many?"

"One," he whispered.

"One. Not five. One. One woman who loves you! How much did I charge you? Nothing! Because everything I am and have is yours. I. Am. Yours! You need to *accept* that, goddammit! I love you and how *dare* you treat that like *shit*?" she gasped. "Like it's nothing!"

Sade grabbed her and pulled her tight to his body, a sob escaping him. "Fuck, Mercy. You're so right. You're so fucking right. I'm fucking confused, I just don't want to hurt you, that's all."

"Then you have to let me help!" she whispered. "I think we did good! I think you did good! I think I did good! Damn you, how can you not see that?"

"Okay baby, I see it. I see, I do. But I hurt you."

"You hurt me?" She suddenly shot out a laugh. And then another. And several more until she was just fucking howling in laughter.

"What the fuck are you laughing at?" Sade asked, sitting up and watching her kick her legs.

"You hurt me," she squeaked, still laughing. She finally looked at him, catching her breath. "You are such a fucking *weenie*, you know that? I mean when it comes to me, you are," she corrected. "Not saying you can't take an ass whipping. But do you have any idea what kind of training my father put me through?" She busted out in snickers again until she was back to kicking her legs.

Sade shook his head in disbelief.

"That was nothing!" she finally said, sitting up and smoothing her hair. "Sade, honestly. Sweetheart. I have spent years learning how to take much more than that. I don't mean this as an insult to your sadism, I swear, but truthfully… my dad prepared me for Armageddon, okay? Years in captivity under torture kind of crazy shit.

"What you just did was rough, yes, but not unbearable. Yes, sex is… a different kind of endurance, I grant you that, but the principal is still there. I just have to break through my tolerance ceiling and move up another level."

Sade was stunned into silence. He didn't know how to respond to that. How to feel about it even. "So what you're trying to say is... you weren't hurt *too* bad?"

"Nooooo, not at all. I'll be sore as shit down there I'm sure, but I'm thinking you will too."

He chuckled with that. "I will."

She shrugged and grimaced while looking at his chest. "You got yourself some nasty scratches to show for it. And hey, if I have to bruise your trachea to help jump start your drive until it starts when I *tell* it... then..."

He looked down and then at her, suddenly overwhelmed with emotion. "Come here," he whispered, holding his hand out to her. She climbed into his lap and he stroked her face and cradled her as she cuddled up against him. "And then you climb into my lap like a sweet angel."

She looked up at him with a smile. "I'm pretty talented."

"You fucking are," he whispered, kissing her nose.

She sucked in a breath and moaned.

"What?"

"Just remembering how you kissed me. Oh my God, that was so amazing."

"I was hungry," he mumbled.

"I like you hungry. You should be hungry like that more often."

"You're asking for my sadism?"

"Ummm. Maybe I'm asking for some of your sadism? Maybe I'm asking for a nice balance. It could be fun," she whispered, stroking his lips with her index finger.

He opened his mouth and bit the tip with a smile. "You're officially the teacher," he muttered. "And I'm your student."

She tilted her head back and puckered her lips with her eyes closed for a kiss. Sade stared at her face, his heart heating again as he leaned in and kissed her puckered lips, softly.

A noise startled both of them and they hurried to their feet. "What was that?" she whispered.

Sade opened the door a little, holding up a hand to her. "Hey Bo, that you?"

At not hearing an answer, panic slammed him. He turned to Mercy and put a finger to his lips, thinking of where the guns were. She nodded and looked around, finding their clothes among the mess, and handing him his. They both quickly dressed and Sade put his mouth to her ear. "I'm checking upstairs first then going down. Stay up here."

She quickly shook her head and mouthed, "I'm going with you."

Fuck he hated this. He shut off the room light and waited in the silence a few moments before slowly opening the door. They checked the bathroom first and found it empty, then Sade looked out of the upstairs window. Not seeing anything, he headed down the stairs with Mercy exactly behind him, one hand clamped on his shoulder, the other in the waistband of his pants.

Sade hoped Bo was just sleeping and didn't hear him call. As they crept through the living room, Sade didn't see anything out of order. Until he saw the trail of blood near the door. Sade crouched to the floor behind the couch and looked around, his heart hammering. Fuck. The guns were in his room he remembered. He needed to get there.

Mercy yanked on him and he signaled for her to stay there while he went to the room for the guns. She nodded, her eyes worried and he signaled for her to be sure and *stay* there. She nodded again.

Sade made the dash to the bedroom and opened the door carefully. His gut twisted at finding the bed empty and blood all over. He glanced behind him, making sure nobody was there before opening the bedroom door all the way. He ventured into the room slowly, looking all around. The bag was in the closet. Fuck. His stomach jerked at regarding the blood on the bed. Where was Bo? What had they done to him?

He put his hand on the closet door just as he heard a brief scream.

Heart hammering, Sade bolted back to the living room and froze at finding the front door open. "Mercy!" He ran for the door then spun at seeing a person in the reflection of the window. A large man stood in the kitchen, wearing a mask with a sad face. Mercy slumped against his leg on the floor, his hand clutching her hair.

Sade raised his hands in surrender, eyeing him.

"Hello Johnathon."

Fuck. Panic pumped hard through Sade. "Do we know each other?"

"Indirectly. Name's Abraham. It's nice to finally meet you."

****

To be continued

My apologies to the fans who expected a longer book. I realized about three fourths of the way through that this story needed more space to tell and decided to make it a duet. So, stay tuned for part two of Mercy~A Dark Erotica, coming in a couple of months.

Come stalk me

Social Media Links

Join my private Dark Erotic Fan Group

Website/Blog

http://lucianbane.com/blog/

Amazon Author Page

http://www.amazon.com/Lucian-Bane/e/B00IZ23JN0/

Twitter:

https://twitter.com/Lucian_Bane

@Lucian_Bane

Facebook:

https://www.facebook.com/author.lucian.bane?ref=br_tf

Lucian Bane's Fan Group

https://www.facebook.com/groups/832495400130628/

Ruin Book series page

https://www.facebook.com/pages/Ruin/1484429548509101

Dom Wars series page

https://www.facebook.com/DOMWars

White Knight series page

https://www.facebook.com/theWKDA

Arks of Octava series page

https://www.facebook.com/pages/Arks-Of-Octava-Bestselling-Author-Lucian-Bane/770705349678836

Goodreads:

https://www.goodreads.com/author/show/7873610.Lucian_Bane

Google+

https://plus.google.com/u/0/+LucianBaneAuthor/posts

Pinterest:

http://www.pinterest.com/lucianbane/

Linked In

www.linkedin.com/pub/lucian-w-bane/a5/658/a2b/

Tumblr

https://www.tumblr.com/blog/lucian-bane

Instagram:

http://instagram.com/lucian.bane.paranormal.romance/

My Facebook Page

More to come

Printed in Poland
by Amazon Fulfillment
Poland Sp. z o.o., Wrocław